FLAP TUCKER: ZEN DETECTIVE

Maytag leaned over to me. "So, Mr. Tucker—you gonna help us find Lydia or not?"

"Did she kill her husband?"

Peachy drew in a big breath through his nose. "We don't really know. She whispered somethin' in his ear, and after he had time to think about it, he just fell over. They tell us he was dead after that. Reckon he got to thinkin' about how bad he'd been—*that's* probably what killed 'im." He stared at nothing for a beat or two. "So how you gonna find 'er, Mr. Tucker?"

Peachy was interested too. "What exactly does a person in your line of work actually *do*?"

I looked out at the golden kitchen. "Often I use the same method that I so successfully employed to find the two of *you*."

Peachy blinked. "What was that?"

"I let *you* come to *me*. . . ."

PRAISE FOR *EASY*, THE DEBUT NOVEL IN PHILLIP DEPOY'S FLAP TUCKER MYSTERY SERIES

"*Easy* is populated with wildly appealing characters . . . and an unusually engaging detective."
—*The Independent Reader*

"A must read for fans of a down-home mystery."
—Harriet Klausner, *Painted Rock Reviews*

"A promising debut in a series that accomplishes the tricky task of being satisfyingly different."
—*Mystery News*

Also by Phillip DePoy

Easy
Messages from Beyond

TOO EASY

Phillip DePoy

A DELL BOOK

Published by
Dell Publishing
a division of
Bantam Doubleday Dell Publishing Group, Inc.
1540 Broadway
New York, New York 10036

The trademark Dell® is registered in the U.S. Patent and Trademark Office.
ISBN: 0-440-22495-0
Printed in the United States of America
Published simultaneously in Canada
August 1998
10 9 8 7 6 5 4 3 2 1
WCD

For Heather Heath,
who looked out the window one fine spring day
and said, "Maybe it would be nice to go to the beach."

For Tracy Devine,
who stood in the snow in Rockefeller Center while
Fletcher and I smoked killer little cigars.

For Frances Kuffel,
who sat in a true Irish pub and
talked about Folly and Taj Mahal.

For S. J. Rozan,
who's cooler than any cold place.

And for the good old Thrower boys
for their story.

CONTENTS

TOO EASY

1

Dinner and Drug Traffic

What do you say to your dinner date when there's a gunshot out the window on a hot summer night?

"'Scuse me, sugar. How's your swordfish?"

You take a look out the window, down to the street. There's a guy with his arm jammed inside somebody's open car door. It's not the first time you've seen this ballet. He's grabbing the steering wheel, shoving it hard toward the curb so the guy in the car can't drive away. He's speaking very calmly for a man in his situation.

"You don't drive away without you give me my money, man—else I take my gun and shoot you and your little dog too."

The guy in the car sees the error of his ways. The car sputters to a halt. Money exchanges hands. You go back to your dinner. The world begins anew.

I don't have that many friends over—a lot of them don't like the neighborhood. Dalliance is the exception—to almost anything. Nobody in the world has a friend like she is to me. We grew up together, starting out down in south Georgia. On this particular evening, however, she found the disturbance in the street annoying.

"Why don't you move?"

"Where?"

"Some quieter place?"

I sat back down. "I always liked the beach."

She took a bite of the swordfish. I'd grilled it on the hibachi out the back window of the spare room. My place is just off Ponce de León, a grand old Atlanta street that we've all agreed to mispronounce. The building's only got four apartments in it. From one end to the other I've got a glassed-in sunroom; a living room where most of the furniture is junk—kind of hobo hip. I've got a fine stereo hidden away; a dining room with a fairly useless bay window—there's nothing to see but the drug traffic; a galley kitchen, although I don't think the apartment would float if it came to it; and two bedrooms. I use one for sleeping, and sometimes the spare room is an office. I have a profession: Flap Tucker, Lost and Found. Plus, it's a great place to barbecue.

Dally took a sip of the wine. It was the 1983 Château Simard—not as good as, say, an '86 Cantenac Brown, which is a wine I would personally pop my own mother for—but the Simard's a steal at twenty bucks a bottle.

She lifted her glass to me. "Try Savannah."

I popped an asparagus in half. "Hmm?"

"Savannah. Tybee Island. It's quiet."

"How am I going to afford a vacation?"

She polished off the wine and reared back in

the chair. "Well, what if it's more like a working vacation?"

I should have known. "You got work for me."

She nodded. "You got a dessert for me?"

"Raspberry Surprise."

"I'll bite. What's the surprise?"

I stood up. "I couldn't find any raspberries so we *got* no dessert. Are you surprised?"

"You're not really much for the sweets, are you?"

I went for another bottle. "I don't see the point."

She went into the living room. "The point is, you get a little denouement. A meal is like a story, pal."

I brought in the new bottle. "I know your theories on the subject. I'd rather talk about this job you think you have for me."

"Oh, I don't *think* I have it—and you're gonna really want to go when I tell you."

"You said that the last time . . . and I still haven't gotten paid, by the way."

She hoisted the bottle out of my hand and gave it a gander. "You don't want for the finer things." She didn't want me talking about the "last time."

I knew what she was doing. She was just trying to get me up and out of the apartment. I'd have to admit I'd been a little sluggish since our last business: a rude little whack name of Lenny—who got away. I mean, we foiled his evil scheme to get rich selling off the sacred treasures of Tibet—but he got away. I hate loose ends. He killed people, I found him . . . and he still got away. I guess I'd have to admit to feeling pretty bad on that particular score.

I settled in across from her. I was in an overstuffed chair that used to belong to my grandmother, who helped to raise me—such as that raising was. She was just about as odd as you'd want to be. She used to get messages from the static between radio stations. Sometimes the message was for her to buy six boxes of Bon Ami cleaner; sometimes the message was for her to take off her clothes and run down the center lane. She also suffered from clinical depression. The sad fact was she wasn't all that unusual in my family. I had a cousin that they locked up and threw away the key, far as I knew. What I'm saying is that I'm the *sanest* one in the bunch—which will give a person the idea of just how much trouble there is in that bunch. My grandmother wasn't even the worst. Still, it was a good chair, and I figured the nut juju was just about gone: she'd been passed away for fifteen years.

I zipped a glance at my dinner companion, then stared into my glass, beaded bubbles winking at the rim. "What's the job?"

"The usual. All you gotta do is find something nobody else can find."

I took a sip. " 'Oh, how feeble is man's power that, if good fortune fall, he cannot add another hour, nor a lost hour recall.' "

"Huh?"

"John Donne."

She blinked. "Okay."

"When you're a layabout like me, you can invest a couple of hours now and again reading poetry . . ."

". . . looking for lines the dollies'll go for."

"Dollies?"

"You heard me. If *you've* got time for poetry, my guess is that it's makin' time for dollies."

I shook my head. "You are one sad setback for the feminist movement."

"Bite me."

"Gladly, but first tell me about the job."

"First tell me about the poetry."

"Brother Donne is trying to tell you that people want the good times to stay—but they don't last. And once they're gone, you can't bring 'em back. I can't find a lost hour, and it's what most people want."

"Don't you get philosophical with me, mister. And I thought Donne was a metaphysical poet, not a pessimist."

I had to smile. She pretends not to know, but she knows. "What's the *job*?"

"You're eager."

"I'm out of cash."

She set her glass down on the table between us. "Two boys, twins, got in a little trouble in Tifton."

"You can't get into *big* trouble in Tifton."

"Be nice. I think I like these boys. Somebody else thinks they killed a banker down there, but they didn't. It was his wife. She's a siren."

I took a bigger sip. "I thought they mostly operated on the rocks wrecking the big boats."

"The boys think she made a sound in his ear that cracked open his skull."

I nodded. "Like a siren."

"Yeah."

"So who's nuttier, the boys or this . . . dolly?"

She smiled. "Hard to say. Do you want to hear more or not? You want me to tell you the story?"

"Do I get to go to the beach?"

"The boys *might* be somewhere on Tybee Island."

"Then I want to hear more." I leaned back in the chair.

Dalliance Oglethorpe—descendant of the founder of Georgia, and owner of Easy, my favorite nightclub in the city—is absolutely one for a story. In fact, she will not give you two cents for a job unless a story goes with it. She's incapable of saying, "Here's the job: Go find some twins." She has to tell you a story with a beginning, a middle, and an end. What am I going to do? I love her, so I listen.

2

A Story

Dally's story went as follows:

There was once a banker who lived in Tifton. He saw a spirit once out on the ocean, and he fell in love with her. She was dressed in white, her hair was gold, and her face was pale and sad. She sat in a golden boat. Night after night he went down and paced the shores and begged her to come onto land and marry him, but she never answered. Finally he called out to her with a promise that a lot of young men make:

"I'll never stop loving you and I'll always be kind."

At that the spirit vanished from the water. There was a musical sound on the rocks, and the woman stepped ashore, followed by servants carrying bags of gold and jewels, her dowry—she was very rich. They married, and were happy, until they went to the christening of a newborn, and the beautiful spirit began to cry.

Her husband was embarrassed. "Stop. Why are you crying?"

"The poor baby. It's entering into a world of great sorrow and sadness. When I think of all the suffering that lies ahead, I can't help but cry."

And in a fit of anger the man shoved her out the door.

She said, "That's once."

It was only six weeks later that the very same baby died, and the couple attended the funeral. Once again the husband was angered by his wife's behavior. She was laughing and singing.

"Hush. Why are you doing that? It's a funeral."

She couldn't help it. "The baby has left this world of sin and sorrow and escaped its misery, how can I be anything but happy?"

And again he reacted in anger, turning her arm.

She looked away. "That's twice."

They lived happily for a time longer, when they were invited to a wedding. Not just any wedding: The husband's boss was marrying a much younger woman. It was widely known she was marrying him for his money. And in the midst of the festivity the spirit burst into tears again.

Her husband was enraged. "What's the matter with you? It's the boss's wedding day."

She wept harder. "When I look at that couple, I know youth is wedded to age for a thing so paltry as gold. They can never be happy."

This time the man exploded, slapping her. "I can't

believe you. Let's get out of here before anyone hears you."

But she was as quiet as a wave. "You've struck me for the third and final time."

And saying that, she whispered in his ear one magic word, and left the place so fast no one could follow. Some ran after her, but all they saw was her golden boat, far out on the ocean. All the banker's wealth—of money and of love—was gone forever. And the banker lay dead on the ground.

3

Beautiful, Georgia

I leaned forward, reaching for the bottle. More wine was absolutely required. "That's your story?"

She let me pour for her too. "That's the way Peachy and Maytag tell it."

"That's the twins?"

She nodded.

I sat back. "How much of it is accurate?"

"All of it. Some bank exec at Tifton Home Loan— one Lowe Acree by name—met a woman when he went deep-sea fishing in Savannah. They got married, he beat her, she killed him, and took it on the lam back home. That's what the boys said before they took off after her."

I nodded. "So why didn't you just tell it to me that way?"

"Don't you go for the folktales?"

I shrugged.

She sipped. "Well, you better get a hold of some,

or you'll never understand those boys. They're a little simple, see—and they love the fairy tales."

"Peachy and Maytag what?"

"Last name of Turner. And it's not actually in Tifton, it's on a farm outside the city limits of Beautiful."

"Say it again."

"Beautiful, Georgia."

"Am I going there or Savannah?"

"Better start around Tifton, that's where the murders took place."

"*Murders?* Plural?"

"Did I happen to mention some of the townsfolk thereabout think the boys killed the banker's wife too?"

"Nice. You don't believe they did."

She shook her head.

"How did you find out about this?"

"Got a friend that teaches at Abraham Baldwin Agricultural College . . ."

". . . in Tifton, Georgia . . ."

She nodded. ". . . and she called."

"What's your friend teach?"

"Metaphysical poetry."

"Shut up."

Dalliance smiled. Whenever she did that, I practically *had* to do what she wanted. She leaned forward. "So, are you going to help me or not?"

"What am I looking for?"

Medium-sized grin. "Churchy la Femme."

"That character in the old *Pogo* cartoons?"

She shook her head. "That French phrase. *That's* the job."

I looked at her. "*Cherchez la femme?* I look for the girl?"

Big nod. "The girl leads you to the *twins*. That's who we really want. Mr. Turner is a *church* member with Sally . . ."

". . . your pal at the agricultural college . . ."

She nodded. ". . . who says he's the nicest man in five states, and *he* wants to hire us to find his boys."

I concentrated. "And you think they might be on Tybee Island."

"Or Savannah, or someplace in between. Mr. Turner's got to know for sure."

"Now it all comes out. And by the way, I thought there wasn't much money in farming these days."

"He's got no money."

That made me sit up straight. "So how does yours truly get paid?"

"Land."

"What?"

"Mr. Turner gives us five-hundred acres of timberland—all old pine. We sell the lumber to somebody, and keep the land to retire on. One day Tifton'll just be a suburb of Atlanta, and we'll be in the catbird seat."

"Whatever that means. And isn't Tifton, like, three and a half, four hours south of here?"

"Uh-huh."

"So what year do you think it'll be a suburb?"

"Oh, not in our lifetime—but our children's children will have something to fall back on."

"Let them fall back on their own petard."

"You can sell your half."

"Done. Like to buy some nice land in south Georgia? It's real hot there, but they make up for it with all the mosquitoes."

"Gnats. And first you have to find the boys."

I settled back again. "First you have to tell me more about the deal."

"The Turner family used to grow tobacco, now it's mostly soybeans, a little feed corn, and cotton's making a comeback—or isn't that what you meant?" She helped herself to a little more wine. "The boys are . . . what are the kind that don't look alike."

"Fraternal?"

"Whatever. They love their daddy, and vice versa, but they're odd boys. Apparently they seem kind of simple when you first meet 'em. Then they'll say something amazing, and you fall in love."

"*You* fall in love. I'm strictly business."

"The whole family's cockeyed, really. They've got an Aunt Ida."

"What's an Aunt Ida?"

"She's a mute who takes care of the family, and communicates with clicks and whistles."

"Like a dolphin."

"By tapping a pencil on the table in her own little code."

"Delightful."

"Didn't you used to have a nutty grandma?"

I patted the arm of the chair I was in. "So?"

"I just thought you'd appreciate these guys. They're a little off, but they've got big old hearts in 'em. They just want to help this girl, who's the real item: seems to come from an old Southern family, big money, overwhelmingly winsome."

"In what way."

"She thinks she's a fish."

"Say what?"

Dally nodded. "She thinks she's a mermaid, a silky, a creature of the sea."

"Get *way* out of here with that."

She leaned forward. "She actually thinks she'll die if she's not near the ocean or something. And I'd take her seriously if I were you. The last guy that made fun of her was her husband."

"Yeah." I slumped down in grandma's chair. "The *last* thing I need is to have somebody whisper a magic word in my ear."

"Right, so . . ."

"Where do I start?"

"Go talk to the dad in Beautiful . . . and Ida if you can. Check out the scene in Tifton; follow the trail to Savannah, if that's where it goes."

"I thought you said Tybee Island, and I don't know if my car'll make it. Do you know what that drive is like?"

"So borrow mine."

"Like that's any better. I'll get a tune-up." I polished off my wine. "What do I live on until I'm a timber baron?"

"Mr. Turner took out a loan against part of the land. You got expenses."

"Happy days are here again."

She stood up. "You need your rest if you're driving to south Georgia tomorrow."

"I hate that drive."

She nodded, took a peep out the window. "What was all the hubbub down there?"

"The gunshot? That's our local pharmaceutical

distributor. He waits on the corner and customers drive by. They hand him money, he gives them what they want, and all's right with the world. Only sometimes they want to drive away without paying. Then he has to explain it to them. Once he shot a guy's tires out."

She closed the blinds. "Call the cops."

"You don't believe in the small business man."

"I just don't want you to catch a stray slug. You got too much lead in your system as it is."

I hoisted myself up from the comfortable chair. "Is that your ever-so-subtle way of telling me I'm lazy?"

"You're the one who said you have time to sit around idly improving your mind. Which I agree could stand the renovation."

I started clearing the dishes. "Look: I call the cops on this guy, he gets the idea I'm the type who likes to do something about it—which we would agree is a false impression. Then he's going to want me to do something with *him,* and I don't even like the guy that much. Live and let live, that's my motto—one of them. Besides, the police're busy chasing the hookers off the street—much easier to hassle, plus *they* don't have guns."

"Flap, you've got a cynical streak through you that, frankly . . . I find enormously attractive."

"Uh-huh."

She held up her hands. "I'm gone. The swordfish was happening. Had a nice smoky flavor."

"You get twigs out of the yard and soak them for twenty minutes, then flop them on the charcoals."

She headed for the door. "Yard twigs. I'll alert the

chef at Cassis." She stood in the doorway for a second. "You're going out of town for a while. I just realized."

I nodded, but I didn't look at her. "*Has* been a while since we were apart like that."

"I don't like it."

I had to look. The light from the hall knocked a halo on her head like a window in church.

"You should stand in a doorway like that more often, Dally. The light's doing you a pretty big favor."

She looked down. "Yeah. I'll miss you, too, Flap."

She checked out. The door closed. It was a little darker in the apartment.

4

Flat

Too early the next morning I found myself out the door and in the street. The sun wasn't quite up, and our curbside entrepreneur from last night was still standing under his streetlamp when it blinked off: the city's equivalent to the rooster.

I waved. "Hey, Horace. Try to keep it down, will you? All the commotion last night scared off my dinner date—and you know I don't have that many."

He looked up. I could see he was tired: long hard night. "Jeez, sorry, Flap. I had a unruly customer. I had to throw a scare into him. You understand."

"Still."

He smiled. "I got more customers than you got dates . . ."

"Lots."

". . . so next time I'll threaten his life with a little more finesse."

I nodded once. "Just quieter would do."

"You got it, brother."

I started to slip into the car, but an idea began to steal into my skull. "Hey, Horace."

He was shuffling his money and was headed for bed. "Uh-huh."

"You sell much weed these days?"

"Some."

"Where's it come from?"

"Flap, you know that's doctor-patient confidential."

"No, I don't mean *who,* I mean *where.* Used to be a truck crop down south when I was a youth."

He was wise. "Oh, yeah. The particular weed of which you speak is still the main cash crop of the wilder boys in our fair state." He closed his eyes. "Sunny south Georgia. It's homegrown, brother— plus: It's organic."

"Skip the sales pitch, Horace, I'm not looking to buy. Just curious."

"You reminisce."

"Occasionally."

He shook his head. "The stuff these kids want today, it's just like takin' a ballpeen hammer and whackin' yourself in the forehead. Not like when you an' me was young."

"What's the big seller these days?"

"Got a new package called Homicide—horse and coke and seasick medicine. Makes you mad as a snake and twice as poisonous."

"Charming. Guess that comes from New York or someplace."

He shook his head. "Lot of it comes from right here in Georgia. Down south."

I shook my head; jabbed the key into the car door. "Look, I may be gone for a while."

He understood. "I see anybody goin' for your stuff, I call the cops." He split a pretty big grin. "I know 'em all."

I didn't doubt it. I'd been seeing Horace on these same streets since 1972. I don't even know what made me try to draw him out that morning, exactly, except sometimes you get an intuition. I nodded, tossed the door open, and shoved myself into the seat. It only took seven cranks and the engine turned over, and by then Horace had vanished. I headed for a grease monkey.

It was well after sunrise on Sunday morning, but I was sole proprietor of the streets. Heading for 75 South, there was a twenty-four-hour BP station close to the overpass on Tenth Street. Alas, no mechanic. It was self-serve. I gassed up, changed the oil myself, kicked the tires, cleaned the windows, and checked the plugs. I knew one of them was bad, but I didn't want to take up any more time to change it then. I just bought a new one and tossed it on the front seat beside me.

I pulled out of the station at eight-oh-five in the A.M. On that same spot had once stood a nightclub called 12th Gate. When I was a callow something-or-other, I played in a little band there. We were the opening act for Elvin Jones and I was too stupid to know what a big deal that was. Now it was a self-serve BP station, and I had no idea where Elvin Jones was. But, I reminisce.

The endless drive down I-75 South has always

been notorious across the United States as the most boring ride in all fifty. Plus, it's hard to drive when you're anxious about the state of your automobile, because there are long stretches of nothing but nothing. I started out with a Coltrane tape in the stereo, but you can only listen to *Giant Steps* about fifty times in a row before you need a change. I was just past Macon, a third of the way, so I twisted the dial on the radio, found what seemed to be the All–Hank Williams Station. It was diverting, but the scenery was still monotonous: it's flat.

Unfortunately my right rear tire was flatter. Just around Cordele I popped a tread. For a major thoroughfare the highway looked a lot like an empty parking lot. I could hear the locusts in the high grass by the side of the road. It was only ten-thirty in the morning, and already over 90 degrees.

It took a little longer to change the flat than it should have, seemed like the nuts were welded on. I figured as long as I was pulled over anyway, I'd change the spark plug, so I popped the hood and went to work. What with the grease and the oil and the heat and all, I was a fine mess when the job was done. And in a dandy mood.

I was just about to close up auto shop when a pickup came into view. I was wiping my hands with a rag when they pulled in behind me.

Two big old boys jumped out, baseball caps and blue jeans. The driver was talkative, jumpy; had the sniffles.

"Need help, mister?"

I shook my head. "Naw. Had a flat. It's fixed."

The other one looked pretty dumb, smiling with his mouth open at the open front of my car. "You ain't got no flat up under 'at hood, bud."

I smiled back. I'm a friendly sort. "Decided to change a plug as long as I was stopped."

The driver crossed his arms. "Welp," sniff, "how about helpin' us out now? We short on cash."

I tossed the rag onto the front seat and put my fist on the door handle. "Can't help you there, boys." I snapped open the door and stepped behind it so it was between me and Bubba.

"That ain't nice. We stop to give you a hand, and you ain't got nothin' for us?"

I raised my eyebrows. "I didn't say that. I just don't have that much cash on me. I'm on my way down to Tifton for a job. Maybe you could catch me on the way back home."

He was edgy. "We can't wait."

He lumbered a step or two forward, and reached out for me with his log-sized forearm, but he was slow and I slammed his arm hard in the car door between us. Then while he was doubled over holding on to it, I bent down and picked up his right foot. The rest of him went down backward like a full sack of feed—it's some kind of law of physics.

His pal didn't move; just stared at the lump on the ground for a minute and then back at me, smiling bigger.

"Tifton, huh? I got kin down yonder. Or in Beautiful, rather."

I reached over to help Bubba up.

He got to his feet, dazed and confused. "I think you broke my arm."

I stepped back from him. "It was probably the car door that did it."

He was still looking down. "I think your car door broke my arm."

His pal actually laughed. "It's you own fault, you moron. What'n this world you wanna hassle some old dude on Sunday morning for?"

This seemed to embarrass the driver of the pick-up. "Yeah. It's my own fault." He looked up at me. He was just a kid. "Sorry, mister. I didn't mean nothin' by it. I jus' . . . I got money problems."

I shook my head. "Let me see your arm."

He held out his hand like a dog, and I felt it all along the wrist to the elbow. "It's the ligaments and muscles got hurt. I don't think the bone's broken, but it's going to hurt for a pretty good while. You got a job?"

"Construction."

"Take a week off."

He took his hand back. "I can't, mister. I got a lit-tle baby on the way, and we don't got the money for hospital."

His friend offered up more sad evidence. "He ain't got no insurance."

Bubba shook his head. "That dang baby stuff— it's gonna cost a whole lotta money."

I eyeballed him, then leaned into the car, reached over to the glove box; pulled a card. "You boys know where the farmers' market is just south of Atlanta?"

Bubba took the card. "Sure. We take mushmelons up 'ere two, three times a year."

I pointed to the card. "Get your wife up to Dr. Thompson, close to there in College Park. It's a free clinic if you take your last tax return to prove you got no money."

He stared at the card. "It's that easy?"

"Yup."

He was suspicious. "Why you doin' this?"

"You need help."

He looked down. "Lord, I sure do. You a doctor?"

I shrugged. "Nope. I just lived in Atlanta a good while now, and I know lots of people. I did this guy a favor once."

The boy looked at me like I was a minister. "Well, you're doin' me a favor now. I don't understand it, but I ain't gonna forget it. What's the name?"

"Flap Tucker."

"Pevus Arnold." He held out his hand to shake before he realized how much it would hurt and took it back.

His friend was laughing again, but he was laughing at me. "You ain't gonna believe this, but my kin down in Beautiful? Is all Tuckers. It's my wife's side. You look up old Rusty Tucker down 'atta way—he set you up with some fine barbecue. Tell him Ronnie Tibadeau said 'hey.' "

I shoved out my lower lip. "I could use some fine barbecue, at that."

"He's the man to see."

I moved to get in the car, and Pevus backed away. He looked over at his consultant. "You drive." Then at me again. "I ain't gonna forget this, Mr. Tucker.

I'm takin' the wife up tomorrow. She six months in and ain't never seen a doctor."

I settled in and slammed the door. Their power pickup roared past me before I could even get cranked. They waved like we'd just been at a picnic together.

5

Snow in Summer

I stopped at the next filling station for more gas, poured down some more oil, and cleaned myself up best I could. I shot a quarter in the phone and rang up Dally collect.

"Hey."

"Flap? Where are you?"

"Nowhere. I just met some boys on the road—an encounter that I am hoping was not a harbinger of things to come."

"What?"

"I was detained by some hick highwaymen."

I could hear her shift the phone to her other ear. I think I'd gotten her out of bed. "You okay?"

"Thanks. I'm fine, but I had to slam a door on a kid's arm."

She yawned. "Well, it's all a part of the show."

"How do you mean?"

"The bold highwayman—it's part of the road thing. Didn't you ever read, like, *Barry Lyndon*?"

"Saw the movie. It was boring."

"Except for the Chieftains' soundtrack."

"Well, yeah—the Chieftains, they're great."

She spoke up. "Well, as you're always mouthin' off to me, there's no such thing as a chance encounter, you know."

"I know."

"So those boys, they've got something to do with something."

I gave her a little laugh. "Nicely put—and you don't have to tell *me* about my Tao. I know all about my Tao, sister."

"Sister?"

"You heard me. Those boys are not at my center. They've got nothing to say to me except maybe where's some good barbecue."

"That's valuable."

"I agree. But it's not germane."

She yawned. I guess I did wake her up. "Well, you never can tell. Just get back on the road. What'd you call me for?"

"To share my experience."

She wasn't going for it. "Uh-huh."

"Okay, the drive is giving me too much time to think. I want you to check on something. See does Tifton Home Loan—that's where you said this Lowe Acree guy worked, right?"

"Uh-huh."

"So, see do they have any affiliation with any other bank or savings and loan in Savannah. Maybe you could call like you're going to open an account, but your family's in Savannah or something and you want . . . I don't know. You say whatever."

"I get it—what's your idea?"

I leaned up against the phone. "No idea. I'm just . . . Quasimodo."

"You got a hunch."

"Yup."

"Terrible joke."

"'Bye, Dally."

"Take care, Flap."

We hung up. Back in the car and headed south; the land got even flatter and hotter. I was between radio stations. It was a long, lonely stretch of road with miles of white on either side. I was going backward in time. It was cotton, lots of it. The boll weevil is a thing of the past—about the only thing that can mess up a good crop now is too much weather. Cotton, when it's close to ready, makes a hot summer field look like snow. So there it was: the snow in summer, the first sign that something was strange. If I'd known then just how much stranger things were going to get, I might have made a U and skittled back home where I belonged.

6

Gold

I drove on through to Beautiful, just followed the
signs. I wanted to get a talk with Mr. Turner. Sunday
morning, I was told, they'd all be in church. I rolled
into the only populated place in town, the Kingdom
Baptist. Looked to me like services had just finished—they go on for a long time in the old primitive
Baptist tradition.

I wasn't even out of the car before some good
soul had my number. "You here for the dinner on the
grounds?"

I cranked myself up from the driver's seat. "Uh-
huh." Stuck my hand out to shake hers. "Flap
Tucker."

She found herself delighted. "You're a Tucker."

"Yes, ma'am."

"Atlanta?"

"It's obvious?"

"Saw your plates."

"Oh."

She took my arm. "I'm a Lee by marriage, but some of us have married Tuckers."

"Should I start apologizing now?"

She slapped my arm. "Oh, they're all good boys in one way or another. I'm Alma."

"Alma. That means 'soul' in Latin."

"Spanish."

"Okay."

She shrugged, dragging me around the building to the yard out back. There were dozens of picnic tables, all laid out with dinner finery, and a crowd of hungry Christians.

She pointed. "There's the Tuckers. They'll be so glad to see you."

"They won't know me. I'm distant."

We'd moved to Atlanta when I was eight. Dally's dad and mine were both looking for better work in the city. I'm not sure they found it. My memories of growing up in this part of Georgia were very slack. I remembered having cousins—one in particular that I played with even before I knew Dally. But she'd gone away. I had no idea where she'd be these days. I didn't even think I'd recognize any of them, or that they'd recognize me. I couldn't really say whether it affected me one way or the other. I really try not to be that big on the family unit, really. Given my family, I thought anyone could follow my reasoning.

I looked at Alma and told her again. "I'm a *distant* type of a relative."

She slapped my arm again. "It's *family*." She squeezed my hand. "They don't treat you right, you come on over to our table."

I looked over the crowd. "Which one's Sally?"

"Gates or Arnold?"

"The one works at the college in Tifton."

"Arnold." She cast an eye about, then pointed. Sally was a fine plump woman sitting beside some of the tastiest-looking fried chicken I'd ever seen.

I angled in that direction. "Look at the sun on that chicken."

She agreed. "Just like a basket of gold."

Sally saw me coming. "You must be Flap."

"I must be."

"Sally."

"Hey."

She stood up. "We've got a lots of Tuckers here today. Reckon any of 'em's kin?"

"Don't think so, but I wouldn't know it if they were. I'm not much on the family thing."

"Oh, it's real big here."

I looked around at the crowd. "I can see that."

"Doesn't mean much to you?"

I couldn't take my eyes off that fried chicken. "You're going to be whoever it is you're going to be no matter who your parents were."

She smiled. It was winning. "*Que sera, sera.*"

"In the words of that great American philosopher, Doris Day."

She was very serious. "Oh, Doris Day's great."

"May we sit?"

"If you think you could eat a bite or two of that chicken you're starin' at, we could sit right here and have us some dinner."

"If it tastes half as good as it looks, I may move down here for good."

She liked that. We sat down and she loaded up a

paper plate. Fried chicken, cutoff corn, black-eyed peas, green beans, fried okra, and boiled squash. I reached for the corn bread myself.

"By the way, Sally, you don't have a boy name of Pevus, do you?"

She clucked. "That boy needs to find his path. He's my nephew on my husband's side. You didn't meet him on the road?"

"Well . . ."

She reached over for her purse. "Lord. How much did he get?"

I took a bite of chicken. "I just gave him some advice is all."

"You didn't give 'im money?"

"Nope."

"Well, that's a relief. I'd hate for you to start off this business thinking bad things about us. Mr. Turner really needs some help."

"It's okay, Sally. So, where is Mr. Turner?"

"Oh, he left after service. He's not much of a socialist since his wife died. He'll be to home, I expect."

"Socialist?" I had to ask.

"He don't socialize at these dinners like he used to. Just comes to church meetin' and then goes on home."

I smiled. "Not much of a socialist."

"Uh-huh, and he's so nice when you get to know him. It's a shame about all this with the boys and all."

"He'll be home all afternoon?"

She nodded. "Their place is close to here."

"Can you point me in the right direction?"

"Eat first, meet a couple Tuckers." She shrugged. "Might be kin."

I nodded. "I'm told Rusty's the one to see for barbecue."

She lowered her voice. "And liquor."

"This is a dry county."

"Oh, yes." She sounded relieved.

"So which one is he?"

She searched her eyes through the gathering, and fixed on one spot, then raised her eyebrows. It's not polite to point.

I saw a happy fat guy talking loud to his cohorts. If we hadn't been at a church gathering in a dry county, I'd have said he was already in his cups.

I took a bite of the chicken leg. "Where's he get his drink?"

She looked down. "Buys some wholesale, makes his own wine—they say it's real good."

"Just wine?"

She thought I was telling a good joke. "You're thinkin' of the mountains, hon. We don't have stills in this part of the country. Everything's so darn flat, we've got no place to hide one."

Arm slapping must be a big thing in a dry county. She whopped my shoulder good.

I was making heavy progress on the meal, but I kept my place in the conversation just the same. "So, Sally—what is it you teach at the college?"

"Poultry science mostly."

"Chickens."

"Well, you've got to factor in your emu and your ostrich nowadays."

"Your *what*?"

"Ostrich." She nodded with confidence. "It's the red meat of the future."

"Really?"

She was vigorous. "Just like a beefsteak with none of the bad fat; some places it sells for twenty dollars an ounce. And you can get a whole lot of meat off one big ostrich."

I tried not to get a mental image. "How'd you and Dally meet?"

She got dreamy. "Dally and Sally—we were interested in the same boy first year of college—when you were off in the service."

"You aren't the one that married that Charlie guy? Was he Charlie Arnold?" Dally'd gone to Wesleyan for a while, and got stuck on a Charlie.

Sally couldn't hide her pride. "You bet."

"So you beat Dally out of the boyfriend."

She settled into her chair, smiling. "Maybe."

"Well, you did or you didn't."

Her voice was softer again, and she wouldn't look at me. "I always got the impression Dally was waitin' for *you* and gave up on Charlie. She didn't hardly talk about anybody else."

"I'm the best friend Dally's got—which'll give you a little idea the kind of *trouble* her life might be in—but that's *it* between us. And I think you won Charlie with this *food*."

Again with the arm slap. "Stop."

"You got Charlie fair and square." I wiped my mouth with the paper napkin. "I'm telling you, it probably had something to do with this chicken, or the cutoff corn."

"I'm proud of that corn. You get a big old boiler;

take it out in the garden, like on a long extension cord? That corn won't leave the stalk till it's in the salty water."

"How do you mean?"

"It's very fresh. You bend the stalk into the boiling water before you even snap off the ear."

I shoved the plate away from me. "Well, it's worth the trouble. I'd marry you for that corn—if you'd have me."

She didn't look at me. She was already thinking about our business. "Okay. Thanks for comin' down to help Mr. Turner. He's a real good man, and he was always nice to us kids growin' up. Once you find the twins, I think you'll see why everybody loves 'em."

"Yes, ma'am." I surveyed my empty plate. "I think I'm going to talk to Rusty for a bit, then I'm going over to the Turner place. Which way?"

She still didn't point. Manners count at church. "You go left out the drive, ride five, six miles out, and catch another left, it's the first big blacktop intersection. Go on down another three miles or so, and their place ought to be on the right. If it's not, you're lost."

"What do I do then?"

"Wave at somebody and ask 'em."

"Wave."

She was serious again. "Oh, you got to wave at folks around here."

"How come?"

"This is a friendly community, Mr. Tucker. If you don't wave, somebody might get the idea you're not as friendly as you need to be, and they take a gun and shoot you."

I stood. "Well, I don't want that."

"No, sir." She stood with me; shook my hand. "Thanks one more time for helpin'. You let me know what's goin' on, now."

"I'll call Dally; she'll call you."

She patted my back. No slapping now. "Good enough. You take care, hon."

I took a last look at that fried chicken. The basket was nearly empty, but all around it there was still a golden light. Maybe the gold wasn't in the food. Maybe it was in Sally Arnold after all.

7

Barbecue

I launched myself off to the loud group of men that had gathered around Rusty Tucker. Then I waved.

They all waved back, some of them even smiled. I fixed a very friendly gaze on Mr. Tucker, the Barbecue King.

"Hey. Name's Flap Tucker."

He was delighted. "Hey, bud—sit on down. We ain't met?"

"No, sir. I live up in Atlanta—have for a good while; not that much in touch with the Tuckers hereabouts."

He nodded. "Happens."

"But on the way down I met an in-law of yours. Ronnie Tibadeau."

He rolled his whole big head. "Oh, Lord. You musta had a flat comin' down here, or some kinda breakdown."

I smiled. "What makes you say that?"

"Onliest way a stranger knows Ronnie, or that

Pevus Arnold, is they got 'helped' on the roadside. How much they get?" He stood, reaching for his wallet.

I held up my hand. "No, sir, Mr. Tucker. Nothing like that. They just needed an obstetrician."

He had no idea what I was talking about. He blinked once and said, again, "How much?"

"Ronnie just told me you were the man to see about some barbecue."

Everybody in the crowd was relieved. Mr. Tucker sat down. "Oh. Barbecue."

He was cautious. "Well, I surely can fix you up. I guess Ronnie wouldna told you 'bout the barbecue if he didn't think you was okay. How much you need, brother? I got it by the gallon or by the fifth."

A fifth of barbecue didn't seem like a colloquialism. It seemed like a code. But I'm pretty good at playing dumb—some would say it's not a stretch.

I looked confused. "I just thought a sandwich and maybe some Brunswick stew."

He leaned forward quick. "Oh. Right. Just a sammich."

The other men were extremely quiet. No eye contact. I decided to let them off the hook. I took a seat across from Rusty and looked at the ground.

"Of course"—I kept my voice low and my eye on the dirt—"I *would* need something to wash it down with."

And the group erupted. Guys were patting my back and Rusty was shaking his head.

He leaned way forward and slapped my knee. "Tha's pretty good, bud. I can fix you up." He looked me up and down. "I surely don't recognize you as a Tucker."

I nodded. "I grew up in south Georgia, but we moved up to Atlanta when I was eight or so." I looked around. "I've still got some cousins drifting around somewhere south of the gnat line. Don't know if I'd remember them or not."

He sighed, nodding. Then, like a rifle shot, his eyes zipped right into mine. "Hey! You ain't that boy had the crazy-ass grandma?"

I had to laugh. "Yeah. That's me. And for the record, the rest of her was pretty crazy too."

He smiled. "That was over . . . where? Around Ideal?"

I smiled back, tried not to lay on the irony too thick. "It was close to Ideal."

"Yeah, your grandma was the only reason the Piggly Wiggly ever even carried Bon Ami cleaner."

I nodded. "That was her brand, when the moon was right."

He leaned back, very happy. "That's right. I heard you was doin' okay up in Atlanta. Man, you come from the *really* crazy side of the family."

I smiled big. "And proud of it."

He looked off; shook his head in a very pleasant way. "Family." Then back at me. "How *is* your grandma?"

I shrugged. "Passed on."

He nodded. "Yeah." More nodding. "So, how you come to know Ronnie? He married my little brother's oldest, you know."

"Well, he did actually stop to 'help' me—him and Pevus. You had it right: I caught a flat. But in the end, they're just good boys—they didn't mean anything. Pevus is the only one that got hurt."

Rusty didn't ask, he just nodded. "Pevus needs guidance."

I agreed. "Well, me too. Who doesn't?"

Rusty leaned way back. "So whatcha down this way for?"

I indicated with my thumb. "Sally Arnold called a friend of mine in Atlanta. She wants me to help the Turner twins."

Somebody in the crowd offered a testimonial. "They good boys. They didn't have nothin' to do with Lowe."

Rusty was my interpreter. "Lowe Acree is the banker got murdered over here at Tifton. His wife killed him and everybody knows it, but Lowe's got a cousin in the law enforcement who don't like the Turners."

I looked up at Rusty. "How come?"

"I don't know, some kinda land deal." He lowered his voice and looked around the group. "Plus, I always thought Tommy was a little sweet on Lowe's wife hisself."

Here and there: an agreement.

"Tommy?"

He nodded. "Tommy Acree, Tifton Police. Lowe's cousin."

"Sweet on Lowe's wife?"

He avoided my eyes. "Some say."

That was it. Silence. I could tell we were about to discuss the weather, and I already knew it was hot.

I stood up. "Well, thank you, Mr. Tucker."

"It's Rusty."

"If you don't mind, I'll be back over this way for a taste one time or another. But I gotta go talk to Mr. Turner now."

He waved. "J.D.'s a good man. Tell 'im I said 'hey.' And you be welcome to some barbecue any old time."

I nodded, and headed over to the car. Sally smiled at me from her table; she was busy setting everybody else up with fine fried cuisine.

The woman who met me in the front yard came steaming up when I opened my door. "You can't leave. You just got here."

"Well, I really came to see J. D. Turner; help him out. They tell me he's at home."

She clouded up on me. "Oh."

"How long are you all usually here for one of these dinners? Maybe I'll make it back."

She shrugged. I didn't get the sudden attitude shift, but I shot out my hand just the same. "Thanks, anyway, Alma."

She didn't shake. "It's Alma *Acree* Lee." And she was gone like smoke.

Wherever you go, people take sides. Without even trying, I had.

0

Crow in the Corn

In less than twenty minutes I was pulling into what I was hoping would be the Turner place. It looked like a lot of other farmhouses: plain white, aluminum siding, one story, kitchen in the center, small front porch. There was a woman in a chair on the porch with a colander in her lap and a paper sack at her feet. She was snapping pole beans.

I got out of the car and she looked up. The thing that made me nervous about most farms like this was the devil dogs they have lying around. These mutts want to eat your liver, it's their only joy. As luck would have it, the Turners kept no dogs.

The woman stopped her work, but didn't get up. I smiled, I waved, I took a step forward. "Hey. I'm Flap Tucker. Sally Arnold sent me over. Is this the Turner place?"

The woman nodded, stone-faced. From in the house I heard an old guy's voice.

"Who is it?"

"It's Flap Tucker out here. Is that Mr. Turner?"

I could hear a rustle and some old-guy noises. Then he appeared in the doorway. I think he'd been catching a nap.

"J. D. Turner. Come up on the porch."

"Thanks." I did.

There were four chairs. One was a rocker, the other three were ladder-backs. I figured the rocker was Mr. Turner's. I flopped down in another, and leaned back on the hind legs until my shoulders were against the house. Mr. Turner rocked and didn't look at me at all. The woman went back to snapping, but wouldn't take her eyes off me.

He gave a little cough. "I appreciate."

I smiled at the woman. Aunt Ida? "Sorry about your trouble."

Mr. Turner let out what, for a guy his size, seemed like a big breath. "Worse trouble ever. An' I's in the Depression."

"Uh-huh. I hope I can help. The boys headed toward the Savannah area, you think?"

He nodded, still focused on something way out in the fields. "They with her." He seemed very sad indeed.

"Her? You mean Lowe's wife?"

He nodded again, like we were talking about the dead.

"What was her name?"

"Lydia. She was a Habersham."

"Everybody seems to think she's the one that killed her husband."

He rocked. "Not everybody. Some that thinks my boys did it."

"Yeah. Lowe's cousin Tommy."

Again with the nod. Ida pulled a pencil out from behind her ear and tapped a couple dozen times on the colander.

Mr. Turner gave me a break. "She says Lowe's cousin Tommy is a Habersham by his mother's side, and it don't pay him to think his own kin did a killin'."

"Does that mean Lowe and Lydia were related?"

Ida tapped again.

Mr. Turner: "Don't know."

I leaned forward in the chair, all four legs on the floor. "What about some land deal Rusty told me about? Rusty says 'hey,' by the way."

"'Hey' to Rusty." He coughed again. "Lowe wanted some land we got that's a ways off. Some kind of chemical dump. Boys didn't wanna sell—not for that."

"Lowe wanted the land?"

"Lowe and Tommy both. They did a lots together. This chemical dump thing was just another money plan. I took it they's mad at the boys not sellin'."

I leaned farther forward. "So what's the truth? Who killed Lowe Acree?"

He looked at me. It was a strong gaze for a man that seemed so weak. "Lowe Acree was killed by his wife, but it was a accident. She got scared, ran off. She's not like other people. My boys went after. They love her like a sister."

Of course he thought that. He was their father. "So why does the law go after your boys?"

"Boys went in to see Lowe 'bout the land. They was in his office when he died. Nobody saw Lydia come in. Lowe was hollerin' at the boys about the land deal, and then Lydia said somethin' to him, whispered in his ear, and he fell forward. Head made a big noise on the dest."

"Desk?" I wasn't certain.

He nodded. "'Swhat I said. And then Lowe's secretary come in, seen nothin' but the boys, and Lowe facedown, some blood, and she called over to the police."

"And the boys split."

He nodded. "They got out right quick."

"An eyewitness all but saw them kill this guy, and they fled the scene."

"Uh-huh."

"Where'd they go?"

"Come home. Had supper. Told me an' Ida what happened. Went after Lydia."

"How'd they know where she went?"

He started rocking again. "Just did."

"When did all this happen?"

"Last Wednesday."

"Now they're in Savannah?"

Ida clicked.

Mr. Turner explained. "She thinks Tybee Island."

"Why does she think that?"

He looked in her direction. "Just does."

I gave up. "I'm told the boys don't look much alike—not for twins."

He agreed. "Some say."

Ida picked up her pencil like she was going to say something else, then put it back behind her ear instead.

I looked at Mr. Turner. "What kind of code is that she uses?"

"She made it up."

"How did you all learn it?" I probably should have known better than to ask.

He looked at me, this time like I was somebody from far, far away. "We family."

That was it. Ida went back to popping beans. Mr. Turner rocked for a while in silence. The silence was good.

Then he patted his leg. "Stay to supper."

"I had a mess of Sally Arnold's fried chicken over at the dinner on the grounds."

He smiled. It was a face that wasn't that used to smiling. "I miss that fried chicken."

"Why didn't you stay after church?"

He looked away again, off into the fields. "Ain't much to mix since the wife died. Tell the truth, half a time I get on back home, forget she ain't here."

"How long's she been gone?"

"Twenty-seven years."

Twenty-seven years an antisocialist, and still forgets the wife is gone. Some broken hearts never mend.

Ida stopped snapping again.

Mr. Turner looked at her, then away, slow. "She died birthin'."

"She died in childbirth?"

They both nodded.

"With the twins?"

Mr. Turner tightened his lips. It seemed like there

was more to the story, but you don't pour your heart out to a stranger—not even a kindhearted schmo like me who only wanted to help.

Finally Mr. Turner got a hold of himself. "Sally tell you about the money?"

"Money?"

"How you get paid."

"Dally said something about how you've got pine trees."

"Uh-huh."

"Plus, you took out a loan?"

"Got the cash. You be need'n' a little travelin' money."

"Yes."

He got himself to his feet. "Come on in the house."

Ida watched me get up. I did everything but wink at her, but she was immune to my charms.

Inside was dark, like a lot of older people's homes. Stuff was boiling on the stove. Good country Southern cooking's only happy if it's been boiled for three days in fat.

Mr. Turner handed me an envelope from the kitchen table. "That's the cash. The rest is in your name over at the Trust."

"You got me a checking account?"

He nodded. In the envelope, there was a big bundle of twenties and a checkbook with my name on it. The balance was written on the front. It was sizable.

"I won't need this much, Mr. Turner."

"Use what you need. Give the rest back to the bank to pay off the loan, let 'em keep a little of the land for the rest of it—everything else is yours."

"None of my business, but can you spare this land?"

He sat down at the kitchen table. "It's the land Lowe wanted to buy—Tommy still does, I reckon. I'd soon give it to you to help the boys." He cleared his throat.

I looked down at the envelope, shook it, then put it in my breast pocket. "So . . . this is from the land Lowe wanted to buy."

He watched me. "Little hot to be wearin' a suit."

I agreed. "But I always try to look my best. I'll need a picture of the boys—what they look like now."

He pulled over a book that was sitting on the table. "This's all I got."

It was their high school annual. He had the page marked with slips of paper.

There they were: two boys that didn't even look vaguely related except for the sweet smile and the names under the pictures.

I smiled back at them. "This is the most recent picture you got?"

He looked up at me. "You help my boys, Mr. Tucker. I can't do without 'em."

His face registered a couple of volumes more on that story. I looked out to the porch. "I'm going to go on and spend the night in Tifton, see can I talk to the bank secretary or maybe even Lowe's cousin Tommy."

He nodded.

"And then I'll get on down Savannah way. I could use me a little seafood."

"I like the scallops. Boys likes the shrimps."

I started out the door. He tried to stand, but I waved. "Keep your seat. I think I can find the car from here."

He waved back and coughed a little more.

Out on the porch Ida was getting up. She was all snapped out. I smiled at her and she whipped that pencil out from behind her ear and did a Krupa on the porch rail. I had no idea what she wanted, but it seemed very earnest.

"Okay, ma'am. Nice to meet you."

From in the house Mr. Turner called out. "She wants me to tell you she's known Tuckers; thinks she knew your kin."

"I don't think so. My kin was from France." I didn't bother to mention that they were Huguenots in America by the time of the Revolution.

Ida shook her head strongly. I got the idea that maybe Mr. Turner wasn't translating everything. She tapped again.

I could barely hear Mr. Turner. "She says she knows what's the truth."

She nodded then, and headed for the screen door. I opened it for her. "You all take care. I'll be in touch."

They both waved, Ida without looking back. I let the screen door close and got down the steps to my car. There was a big black crow out on the edge of the corn in their kitchen garden. I thought about Sally's technique of fresh corn; paid no attention to the crow. Maybe I should have, but you can't think that every little thing is a sign, even if it is. That kind of thinking will make you paranoid, and that's the last thing you need in my line of work, where everybody and his brother's got something against you just because you're there. On the other hand, as the joke goes, just because you're paranoid doesn't mean they *aren't* really out to get you.

9

"Countin' Flowers
on the Wall..."

I was over at the Tifton Motor Inn within the hour.
In just about that amount of time I had Dally on the
phone again, telling her the events of the day. She
was confused.

"This is worse than a Russian novel trying to
keep up with these names."

I tried to help. "It's not that hard. Everybody's a
Tucker or a Turner—or an Arnold."

"Or a Tibadeau or an Acree or a . . . what was
the woman that ended up hatin' you because you're
there to help the killers?"

"She's a Lee by marriage, but she *was* an Acree,
and that's what counts."

"I can't keep it straight."

"You don't need to. By the way, what about you
and Charlie Arnold?"

"What about it?"

"Sally said you were sweet on him."

"Sally was sweet on him. I was saving myself for Mister Right."

"Then this'll hand you a laugh. She thinks you were waiting for me."

She didn't laugh. "I was just waiting."

I let it go. "Well, Mr. Turner seems a little on the frail side. And Aunt Ida is leaky in the brain pan."

"She just can't talk."

"Oh, there's way more to it than that. Her little Morse code is quirky, wouldn't you say? Plus, I believe she tried to tell me something that Mr. Turner didn't want me to know."

"Like what?"

"I have no idea."

"Yeah, well, then . . . get some sleep tonight. Call me in the afternoon. I'll have had time for that banking business by two o'clock."

"I hope I'll be in Savannah by then."

"You get to go to the beach. I'm envious. By the way, I made you a reservation at the DeSoto Beach Motel on Tybee."

"I know it well. Musta been hard to get this time of year on such short notice."

"Professional courtesy."

She amazed me. "Is there anybody in the state who doesn't know you?"

"Nobody worth knowin'."

I missed her already. "You know, I'd really rather just be hogging a barstool at Easy."

"You're goin' to the beach. That's where I'd rather be."

"Uh-huh. I have to drive for hours in my hot,

sticky car while you get to lounge around in your
nice cool nightclub. Who's playing tonight?"

"We're closed. Air conditioner's on the fritz."

"A likely story. I been in your joint when it was a
hundred and fifty degrees."

"Still, we're closed."

"What's up, Dally?"

"Say good-bye, Flap. I got some work to do."

"Okay."

We hung up. I let my eye wander about the room:
flowered wallpaper and two standing lamps. Aside
from the bed I was lounging on, there was a closet, a
chest of drawers, and a little tablelike desk. As luck
would have it, there was also cable TV and an old
movie channel. I was tired from all the driving, and
still full from the dinner, so a little lying around
watching old movies seemed just right. Kept me from
thinking too much about anything.

10

The Trouble with Banks

I got up early Monday morning; thought I could hit the bank first thing. I stepped out my door at the motor inn and saw somebody waist deep in my open hood, clunking around to beat the band.

"Morning."

A silence fell under the hood. Then: "That you, Mr. Tucker?"

Who should emerge but one Ronnie Tibadeau, yielding a socket wrench, greasy and grinning like a gibbon.

"Ronnie."

"Hey."

"Lose something?"

He looked back at my engine just to make sure. "Oh, no, sir. I just heard the way you was havin' trouble crankin' yesterday, and it sounded like a carburetor problem—which it was. So . . . you all set now."

"You fixed my car?"

He grinned even bigger. "Well, naw. Thas' gonna take a ton more work."

"And a bigger hammer."

"Right."

"But you fixed the carburetor?"

"Uh-huh. She crank right good now, I believe."

I buttoned my suit. "What do I owe you?"

He started backing away. Maybe he was shy, or maybe he was afraid I was going to get him close to an open car door. "You don' owe me a thing, Mr. Tucker. Peach and Maytag, they my buds. Plus you was awful nice to Pevus, considerin' the situation. I . . ." But he couldn't put the rest into words. "It's like a honor to help."

I moved toward the car, slammed the hood down. He backed up another step. "Well, you *know* what's wrong with you kids today?"

He was eager to hear. "No, sir. What?"

I gave him what I thought was a very friendly wave. "Nothing I can tell." I got in the car. "Take it easy." And my old heap turned over on the first try. I don't think it had done that since I bought it.

The bank was only a couple of blocks away. I shoved the door a little harder than I needed to, and it made a racket. There was nobody much in the place yet. A couple of tellers were getting the money ready, or whatever it is tellers do first thing. I sauntered over and gave it a shot.

"Hey." I waved.

One waved back. "Morning."

"Which one was Lowe's secretary?"

They both locked eyes on me. The one who waved stood up. "It's Connie."

She indicated with her head a small woman in front of the biggest office in the place. I could see, in front of the office, a portrait of a man posed as Southern aristocracy, and it had flowers all around it. The late Lowe Acree, I presumed.

I headed for Connie. She saw me coming.

"Hey, Connie. I'm Flap Tucker. Could I talk to you about this mess with the Turner boys?"

"You're a policeman?"

"No, ma'am."

She squinted. "Well, what do you want, then?"

"You saw the boys do it?"

"What do you want?"

Somebody came out of the office, and the security guard was ambling my way.

The guy from the office must have been the one in charge of foreclosures. He wanted me out right away. "You'll have to leave now if you're not a policeman. There's been enough publicity about this already."

"I'm not a reporter."

"Really." He didn't believe me.

"I'm helping Mr. Turner out. He just wants to know where his boys are."

That stopped him. "Well, me too." But he was mean about it.

Connie looked oddly relieved. "You're helpin' J.D.?"

"Yes, ma'am."

Neither my manners nor my helpful nature cut

any mustard whatsoever with the office guy. "I don't really care who you're here to help. Unless you're opening an account, I'll have to ask you to leave."

He lifted his head to the security guy, who actually put his hand on his gun and stepped up right beside me.

I kept my eye on the office guy. "As it happens, I already *have* an account here. I'd like to cash a check."

Very carefully, showing the young and nervous security guard exactly what I was doing, I unbuttoned my suit coat and took out the checkbook in the breast pocket. I dangled it in the air like a little fish.

Office Guy was peevish. "Name."

"Flap Tucker."

He rolled his head. "We'll check." And he lumbered over to the nearest computer terminal. Apparently everything was in order, because he just got madder.

"Amount."

I reached for the pen on Connie's desk. "Twenty thousand dollars."

His eyes shot up from the monitor screen. I made as to write the check. He took a step toward me.

"We . . . that will almost close out your account—and of course an amount of that nature would require a little notice or a cashier's check."

I started to fill in an amount. "I *want* to close out my account here—you're not friendly. I want cash, I don't trust your cashiers or their checks, they're not very friendly either."

He was coming over to me and brushing the security guard aside. "We're not prepared to offer you that much cash at this moment."

"You're not *offering* me anything, I'm just taking my own money out of your cheesy little bank and giving it to somebody who's a little more courteous."

Connie sat down, trying not to smile. I smiled back at her, and she looked up.

"Are you kin to Rusty Tucker?"

"It's possible."

She looked real close at my mug. "Did I see you yesterday at the dinner meeting?"

"At the Baptist? Yes, ma'am."

I finished making out the check and handed it to Office Guy. He didn't even look at it. He was still staring at me and trying to explain the rules of our national financial institutions.

"FDIC only really allows us a maximum cash transaction—"

"Don't you be spelling things out to me, pal. Just how much do you think your dinky little operation here *can* manage?"

He looked at the check, started to hand it back to me, and tell me to take it to the cashier's window, but then he saw I'd only made it for a couple hundred, and I was continuing my conversation with Connie.

"That Sally Arnold sure is nice."

Connie agreed. "She's real smart too. I bet she told you about ostrich."

"Yup."

"Won't stop talkin' about it."

"It's the red meat of the future."

"We keep goats."

"Now, Connie, there's some that think it makes a good barbecue, a goat, but legally barbecue is only pig. The rest is just some kind of meat cooked outside and ought not to be called *barbecue* at all."

"You sound like my husband."

"That lucky man."

She giggled like a kid, which she was far from. "Stop it."

"Okay."

"But Sally *is* nice. She's one of our best volunteers at the church."

I nodded. "She's got a good nature. She's the one called me in to help find the Turner boys."

Connie looked away. "She would. She always wants to help."

I lowered my voice. "Sorry, Connie, but what about seeing the boys in Lowe's office?" I nodded toward the picture in the flowers. "That him?"

She nodded, lowering her voice to match mine. "By the time I came in, Lowe was . . . gone. But I heard him yelling at the boys?" Almost a whisper: "Telling them they were *retarded* and all . . . which they're not."

"They just didn't want to give him that land."

"Right."

"But he was loud."

"Uh-huh. He yelled a lot. Lost his temper somethin' awful."

"And then you heard a bump or something."

I could barely hear her. "It was like somebody dropped a big old rock on the desk."

"And then you went in?"

"I thought Lowe had thrown something at the boys. But then it was real quiet, and Peachy hollered out, said come in quick, and there was Lowe. It was . . . a mess."

She had to quit talking. Office Guy, dumb as a stump, was still standing there with the check in his fingers. "You don't have to say anything to him, Connie."

She looked at me again. "It was awful."

I looked over at Office Guy. "Got my cash yet?"

"Oh." Before he could think, he headed off to the cashier's window.

I returned to Connie. "You don't think the boys did it."

"They said Ms. Acree had come in—his wife? But I didn't see her. She was a very different sort of a person. I'd just as soon believe she did it . . . and I wouldn't blame her." Once again with the lowered volume, this time more intense. "He used to hit her—even in public."

"What for?"

"He . . . not to say anything bad about him, now, because he's dead and all, but he was just plain mean. He was a very violent man, even at work, but especially in the evenings. You just never could tell what he might do."

"To everybody."

She nodded; looked down. "Mostly to women."

He must have been a swell boss to have. "You don't know if they did an autopsy, do you?"

"No. I mean, I don't know if they did or not."

"Okay." I smiled at her. "Thanks, Connie."

She gave me a little nod, like a period at the end of a sentence. Then she leaned real close. "Peaker Brothers might know."

I leaned in too. "Who are the Peaker brothers?"

"Morticians."

"They're here in town?"

"Just down the block."

Office Guy was back. "Here." He handed over the cash.

I stood, still looking at Connie. "That was quick—but I'm still changing banks."

He didn't care. "You do that."

I shot him a look that's supposed to mean something in French. I got the impression he didn't speak any foreign languages, but he understood me well enough.

Still, I had to ask. "You don't know me. Why, exactly, are you such a firecracker?"

He was plain. "I just don't like troublemakers."

I stuck out my lip. "Seems to me there's already been enough trouble to go around, but I believe it started since way before I got here."

"Well, it was those retarded Turner twins killed Lowe Acree—and I don't like the idea of you or anybody else helping them get away with it."

Connie's voice was very even for a change. "This is Byron Lee. I believe you met his wife yesterday at the dinner. She used to be an Acree?"

I got it. "You're *Alma*'s husband."

He bobbed his head once; it was more like a punch in the face than a period in a sentence.

People will tell you it's a small world, but it's not.

It's a great big old world, only it's filled with a lot of small towns.

I put the cash in my pants pocket and smiled at Connie. She smiled back, gave a look at Alma's husband, and stopped smiling. I waved at the security guard on the way out. He didn't wave back.

11

The Trouble with Mortuaries

The Peaker Brothers' establishment was a grand old Confederate mansion–looking place with a square black sign out front: Peaker Family Mortuary, Caring Since 1934.

Inside, the climate control was cranked to the maximum and the air was filled with the scent of jasmine. No one came to the entranceway, so I looked around. I'd never been inside a mortuary before— although I'd known morticians. They always seemed to me to be detached from a normal relationship with reality.

I've made the mistake in my life of reading a lot of books on world religions, and the Buddha tells us that a sort of nonattachment is a good way out of the troubles in this world. But then he also says you're supposed to have compassion all over the place. The only things I've ever had any kind of passion for at all were the things that I'd formed an attachment to. Either you care or you don't. I mean, why do you think Jesus wept, anyway? I always thought it was because he was supposed to have cared.

I was looking up at a picture of Jesus holding a lamb, looking very much like he cared, when dulcet tones floated through the air behind me.

"Jesus wept."

I turned to face him. "I was just thinking about that."

He was late twenties, bald, and kindly. "Jesus wept when he lost even one lamb. It hurt him to see any sorrow. Let him be your rock."

"Okay."

That seemed good enough for him. "Porter Peaker. How may I help?"

"You and your brother took care of Lowe Acree."

"We did."

"Was there an autopsy, do you know?"

"Oh." His demeanor relaxed. "Newspaper?"

"What makes you say that?"

"If you were a policeman, you'd already know that Lowe's cousin, Tommy Acree, would not authorize an autopsy. He's a policeman himself, and he's got ways."

Ways of *what* we didn't get into. "Somebody told me he was sweet on Lowe's wife."

He nodded. "Some say. I wouldn't know. Is that what you wanted to ask?"

I shook my head. "So, no autopsy?"

"No autopsy."

"Any special . . . circumstances of the body?"

"Are you a reporter?"

"Nope."

"Tell me the truth."

I stuck out my hand. "I'm Flap Tucker from Atlanta. Sally Arnold over at the college called me in to help out J. D. Turner. He can't put his hand to his boys right now."

"You're here to help the Turner twins?"

I couldn't tell from his expression which side of the issue he came down on. I had guessed by now that nearly everybody in town would come down on one side or the other. He kept his eyes on me and called out over his shoulder. "Pyle?"

From a room deeper in the mortuary, I heard another voice. "What?"

"Would you come out here, please?"

After a couple of seconds there was another Peaker. The family resemblance was unmistakable. The Addams Family had moved to Mayberry.

Porter explained things to his brother. "Says he's here to help the twins."

Pyle nodded. I didn't know if I was about to be taken into a confidence or thrown out on my leaden backside.

They motioned me back to an office. I followed, but I was on my guard. I think I could have taken them in a fair fight, but they had needles and scalpels and God knows what else on their side.

We all sat. Pyle was the first to explain. "We're not doctors."

Porter chimed in. "But we're quite knowledgeable."

Pyle continued. "We think Lowe Acree had an aneurysm."

Porter agreed. "And it caused heart failure."

I sat back. "What makes you think all this?"

Pyle was first. "Three things." He held up three fingers to prove it. "First, the Turner twins are incapable of hurting anyone."

This worried Porter. "But that's not very scientific."

Pyle was undaunted. "No, but second, the bump on Lowe's head was not a bad one, and could not possibly, all by itself, have caused anybody's death."

Porter was more satisfied with this line of thinking. "When you've seen as many bodies as we have, you get to know a thing or two."

Pyle nodded. "And three: There were no other bruises or wounds or scratches or anything anywhere on Lowe at all. Not anywhere. A little discoloration on his throat, but we think his neck was swollen after he passed out and his collar and tie choked him."

Porter wanted to make it clearer. "How did the Turners crack him on the head without touching him? No weapons. No sticks. No anything. Lowe hit his head on the desk."

Pyle was satisfied. "He fell forward and hit his head on the desk. He was already dead. Everything about that body said heart attack to me."

Porter was happy to agree. "Me too."

I understood. "And when you've seen as many bodies as you all have . . ."

They smiled.

Porter leaned forward. "We buried Lowe Acree in boxer shorts."

I was temporarily at a loss.

Pyle giggled like a kid. "Big white boxer shorts with red hearts . . . and Dalmatian dogs all over them."

Porter tapped my leg. "That way, if they exhume the body anytime soon, we'll have an opportunity to say we had some suspicions about a heart attack."

Or a Dalmatian dog attack, but I resisted the urge to mention it.

Pyle sighed. "Also, we thought it would cheer Tommy up."

Porter settled back. "He's so distraught." He looked at me very genuinely. "It's our job to make people feel better. We thought it would help lighten his load."

Pyle shook his head. "But I don't think he understood me when I told him about it—the boxer shorts—at the funeral? He just looked at me for a long time and then said he'd send us a check."

I smiled. "Why are you telling me this?"

Porter offered. "We went to grammar school with Peachy and Maytag. They're good boys."

Pyle qualified it. "Not to say they're not a little strange in their ways . . ."

Porter was undaunted. ". . . but I'll tell you what's the truth: They never killed a fly—let alone a banker."

Just to keep things straight, I had to ask. "Who did kill Lowe Acree?"

Pyle, in what I took to be an uncharacteristic bit of bile, made a mean noise. "I don't know, but if I'd been there, I might have helped."

Porter explained. "We went to school with Lowe too. He was always a bully." He lowered his voice. "He beat Pyle up two days in a row once."

Pyle tightened his lips. "Him and three of his friends."

Porter looked down. "I was home with the measles."

I looked at Pyle. "What made him quit?"

Porter answered. "I got over the measles and went back to school, that's all. He'd never gang up on the two of us. He was a bully *and* a coward."

You had to wonder if maybe that episode hadn't had something to do with burying the guy in humiliating underwear. Morticians' revenge.

Pyle stood. "I've got to get back to work. I'm happy to have met you. I hope you can help the Turners."

I stood too. "I hope I can *find* the Turners."

Porter joined us out the door. "Oh, they're not smart enough to hide all that well. You won't have much trouble."

Pyle stood in the doorway to his workroom. "Old Mr. Turner must be worried sick."

I had to agree there. "He seems kind of sick anyway."

They nodded solemnly. It was a fine example of professional synchronized sympathy. Porter broke the silence. "He hasn't been the same since his wife died."

It was obviously something they'd heard everybody say. They weren't old enough to know what he was like before she died.

Just at the door, back out in the heat, I turned to Porter again. "Any idea how I can get ahold of Tommy?"

"Police station's right there at the town square." He pointed. "Can't miss it."

"Thanks."

He closed the door behind me. I got the impression they were the sort of morticians that played jokes on each other in the middle of the night, putting the stiffs into funny positions to crack each other up, sitting the bodies up in each other's offices when nobody was looking, generally playing around. I think it was right about then I decided to have my body cremated.

12

The Trouble with
Police Stations

The police station was nearly as cold as the mortuary, but a lot brighter and noisier. There was a very cheery young woman at a desk just inside the front door.

"Hey. What can I do you for?"

I resisted any sort of *urban* comeback to the question. "Looking for Detective Tommy Acree."

"Well, he won't be hard to find." This was a good joke to her. "He *works* here."

I played along. "That *will* make it easier. Think he's in?"

She sang out. "Tommy?"

There was a voice down the hall. "Doe-reen?"

"Somebody's here to see you. Are you in?" She winked at me.

"Send 'em back."

She pointed; I smiled at her. "Nice intercom system."

She got another laugh. I headed down the hall. First door on the left and there was a guy behind a desk sipping coffee and motioning me in.

Before I even sat down, I thought I should make matters clear. "Name's Flap Tucker. Mr. Turner has hired me to find his boys. I was just hoping I could ask you a few questions."

He set his coffee down on his desk and I was a little surprised to see him stick out his hand.

I shook it. He talked. "Welcome to Tifton. How'd you like Sally's fried chicken?"

I understood. He was telling me he already knew everything about me. "I liked it fine. Good cutoff corn too."

"She's got a secret method."

I sat. "The extension-cord method. We discussed it."

He leaned back in his chair. "Sally's a fine woman and we all think the world of her, but as you might imagine, we've got a whole lot of people around here already lookin' for Peach and Maytag Turner."

"Yeah, but Mr. Turner's worried."

"Mr. Turner's worried because of my . . . relationship with Lowe Acree and his wife. He thinks the boys won't get a fair shot."

"But they will."

"From me they'll get the same treatment I give to any criminal."

"I see."

"So your help is most likely not needed."

"Still, Mr. Turner's paying me, and I don't like to take the money and run."

He sighed. "If you interfere with our investigation, I'll put you in the jailhouse."

"I'm very big on noninterference."

"I hope so."

I looked around his office. "You don't want to see my P.I. license?"

He sighed again. "You're a licensed private investigator?"

"Uh-huh."

"You're not a friend of the family?"

"Well, I am now."

"Are you related to our Tuckers hereabout?"

"I could be."

He considered. "Well, Rusty Tucker is a friend of mine, and I'd like to keep it that way."

"Me too." But I had no idea what he was getting at.

"You're from Atlanta?"

"Yes."

"Work there?"

"Often."

"I see." I think he was understanding something about me that may not have been accurate, but I wasn't going to argue, because it looked like it was helping.

I sat up. "I guess you'd have to say that Lydia Acree is missing too."

His face was a block of marble. "Uh-huh. I'll find her."

"You don't think she's dead?"

"I pray to God she's not."

"But there are those in town that believe she's another victim of the Turner killing spree."

"There are those."

I hesitated. "What's she like?"

This irritated him. "What's she like? What kind of a question is that?"

I didn't know what kind of a question it was, but it obviously meant more to him than it did to me. "I was just wondering."

"Well, I'm pretty busy now. You'll have to excuse me." He stood up, visibly agitated, to usher me out the door. "But before you leave, I *will* have a look at that license—and we'll be taking your fingerprints too. I'd like to have them on file."

I couldn't figure what had gotten him so instantly riled. I kept my seat. "My fingerprints are already on file with the licensing bureau in Atlanta. You can send for a copy."

"I'd like to have some originals."

"Make up a charge, get a warrant, find me, arrest me, and book me—then you can have some originals. Until that happens, I'll be on my way." Then I stood up.

He took another step. He was inches from me. "I'll be looking at your gun registration too."

I didn't move a muscle. "Don't carry one."

"Is that right?" He reached around behind him and pulled out his own gun—not to point it at me, just to show it to me. "Does this one make you nervous?"

"Nope."

He tried his best to sound tough. "It ought to."

I stuck my face even closer. "The last time I was afraid to die was over twenty years ago—I was quite young."

He smiled. "Oh, I could do lots worse things with this gun than kill you."

"No you couldn't."

"You don't think so?"

I shook my head. "Nope. Because if you started something, you'd have to kill me. I wouldn't quit coming till you did. You can take *that* to the bank you got down the block." Things were very tense for a second. "And while you're there, why don't you run up an alley and holler 'fish.' "

He was momentarily discombobulated. "What?"

"You heard me."

He busted out laughing. "Yeah. I heard you. That's from the *Andy Griffith Show*."

I nodded, stepped back; relaxed. "It was Gomer."

"Says it to Barney in the 'Citizen's Arrest' episode."

"Right."

He put his gun away. " 'Run up an alley had holler *fish*.' What a stupid thing to say."

I relaxed. "Always handed me a laugh."

He was with me. "I love that show."

"Me too."

He actually patted my back. "Well, Flap—you're a tough guy."

I disagreed. "No such thing. I'm a layabout."

"I guess you get to watch a lotta TV in your line of work."

"A fair amount."

He patted me again. "You really related to Rusty?"

"Any Tucker's a Tucker, I guess."

"Well, don't get in my way on this thing, Tucker or not. I'll snap an obstruction-of-justice charge on you like a bat on a cow's neck. Then you could spend some time in our little lockup here." Smile chiseled out of a big block of ice. "Otherwise, help yourself.

We'll get to 'em before you do anyway. It'll be some easy money for you."

"Yeah. It's been easy so far."

"Got any leads?"

"Where would a guy like me get leads?"

He looked at me sideways for a while, then let it go. "See you."

I headed out the door. "Hope not."

He stood in his doorway watching me leave. I had planned to stop and ask the perky secretary about Lydia Habersham, but the cold eyes of the law would have none of it.

I bumped out the door and into the rising heat; headed back to my car. I'd talked to a lot of people, and gotten a lot of opinions, but I didn't seem any closer to the truth.

13

Silver Queen

I decided to try for Savannah before the heat got really brutal. The drive over from Tifton's not so bad if you don't mind the scenic route. You get to go by a lot of farms and in the summer the corn is as high as an elephant's eye. This has always been a surreal image to me: an elephant in a cornfield. Gave me nightmares as a kid. Why did they write it that way? Why couldn't the corn be as high as the Fourth of July? Corn tassels even look like fireworks. But, I reminisce.

I got back to the car, and this time there was a dead body under it. Only when I made a noise, the legs wiggled and Ronnie Tibadeau squirmed out from under.

"U-joint's greased." He got himself to his feet. "Plus, I took care of everything else."

"Everything else?"

He looked back at the car, to make sure it was still there. "Yeah. Everything else, you know . . . plus, it's all good to go now."

No idea what *everything else* entailed, but I'm not that mechanical. "Ronnie, you're going to town on this car. What's the deal?"

"Got nothin' better to do."

"Pevus take his wife up to the doctor?"

Ronnie nodded. "Thas' where he is now."

"Did you do anything else to the car I should know about? Supercharge it, bore out the cylinders?"

He grinned. "Naw. I knew you was goin' to Savannah, so I thought she might need a little work—you know."

"Well." I mean, what can you say? I didn't even feel like asking *how* he knew where I was going. "By the way, does everybody in the *world* know that Peach and Maytag went down Savannah way?"

He looked down. "Aw, I reckon there's some that don't know it. I hear they got a lots a people over in China."

"Yeah. They do."

"Have a good trip."

I opened up the door and he stood back. This time I was certain he was standing clear of it, but maybe it was just an automatic response. I smiled at him. "*Peachy* and *Maytag*. That's some strange names for a couple of farm boys, don't you think?"

This was the biggest joke he'd ever heard. "You got a name like *Flap* an' you wanna ast me that?"

"Okay." I shoved the key in the ignition and it roared right up. "You got me there."

He waved. I pulled out. Farewell, Tifton.

Now, as I was saying, the corn was up and tasseled. I've got a romance with corn, especially Silver Queen. It's probably primal. About the time of my youth I was reading too much world religion, I also got hooked on mythology. In a couple of native American cultures, corn is responsible for the creation of human beings. I don't know all that much about my family history, but I could believe corn somehow played a part. Doesn't stop me from taking a bite out of a roasted ear if I get the chance.

Eventually, though, the cornfields pass and the air begins to fill up with the sea, and the sulfur, the awful hellish smell from the paper mill; and the Spanish moss hangs low, and the big white cranes balance on one leg in a marshy lowland, and you're nearly into the city.

Savannah's more gothic than Charleston, in the Romantic sense. And it's more urbane than any coastal city in Florida. Parts of the port look like New Orleans—parts look like Hell on a bad day.

Down on River Street, where the big boats come in, there used to be a place called the Night Flight Cafe, where I played when I was the aforementioned callow something-or-other. Jazz with a little *j*. The big hit for us was an old Cab Calloway tune, "Minnie the Moocher," all about a frail dame—something of a Silver Queen herself, now that I think of it, though by no means to imply that the song itself is corny—who was in love with a guy named Smoky Joe, a coke-head. In my youth, I could *hi-de-ho* till the cows came home. But the Night Flight's gone now.

River Street's looking fair, though. It's a great place for the tourists. So is the historical district.

Got a lot of swell bed-and-breakfast joints. For me, it's all too far from the sea. If I'm that close to the beach, I want to be able to roll myself out of bed and down to the water without actually having to get up off the ground. That's why you have to go to Tybee Island.

14

Stardust

It always seems like a long drive out a two-lane with marsh and seawater on either side, but once you're on the island, it's worth it. The first big place you come to after the turn in the road is the DeSoto Beach Motel. It was probably something in the big-band days. I think there used to be a dance-hall pier out on the water where all the greats played: Ellington, the Dorsey brothers, Glenn Miller. Now it's kind of weedy and nobody much goes there, but the ambience is just right for me, and all that great music—melodies of days gone by, like "Stardust"—all on the jukebox in the lounge.

I pulled into the gravel parking lot. It was just as I'd remembered it: big, clunky, beautiful, and nearly empty. Checking in was a breeze, Dally had made all the arrangements. I had what amounted to a suite, which only meant there were two rooms together with a kind of sitting room in between, but it was up high and there was a bay window overlooking the

beach. After I threw my junk in the closet, and un-
packed a very important grocery sack, I gave a call
down to the concierge, just for laughs.

"Hey, Flap Tucker, Room Twenty-seven. I was
just wondering if my friends had checked in yet."

"I'll be happy to look for you, Mr. Tucker. What
were their names?"

"Turner."

She checked. No Turners yet. She checked some
more, and seemed worried. "Um, Mr. Tucker? We
don't seem to see any reservations under *Turner* for
this week at all."

"No kidding. Maybe I better give 'em a call at
home. Could you give me an outside line?"

"Surely."

And there was an instant dial tone. I tried the
same trick with the three other hotels on the island.
No dice. The boys weren't in a hotel on Tybee, or
else they weren't as simple as everybody thought and
had used another name. It was worth a check,
though; it gave me the sense of having done a little
work. So I felt I deserved a break. I shuttled myself
down to the lounge with the grocery sack in my
arms.

The lounge was just what a good bar ought to be.
Kind of small, a little dark, not so clean that you
were nervous about spilling anything, and loaded up
with atmosphere. I jammed myself onto a barstool
and conked the sack onto the countertop. The mistress of the establishment approached, a fine, handsome woman in her early fifties, long straight gray
hair that somehow actually made her look younger.

"What can I get for you?"

I shoved the sack her way. "In here there are three bottles of the famous 1983 Château Simard. I would like to drink them all, but I would like to do it in these very pleasant surroundings. And despite the fact that they're already bought and paid for, I will tip generously anyone who would not only open, decant, and pour this stuff for me, but guard it so nobody else gets any. It's not that I'm greedy, but this is the only sort of wine I can stand to drink, and you've got so much other stuff here for everybody else. If I go sharing my particular poison with all and sundry, by and by it's all gone. Then I'm unhappy, and the generous tips evaporate, you understand. So I'm asking, could we make an arrangement?"

She had to laugh. "You must be Flap. Dally said you was a character."

"And she was right." I'm never surprised anymore when somebody I meet knows Dalliance Oglethorpe. She gets around plenty—plus, she's in the bar business, and it's a kind of network, or family, like any other. Lots of people know about her joint, Easy. It's a home away from home for a brace of oddballs. And anybody that knows Dally loves her—you'd have to be crazy *not* to be crazy about her.

The barkeep stuck out her hand. "It's June."

"Hey, June. So Dally called you about me."

She nodded. "Said you'd be down. Told me to help if I could."

"Can you?"

"Sugar babe, there ain't a thing that happens on this island I don't know a little somethin' about. Not to mention I'm clairvoyant."

"Is that a fact?"

"Yup. The very first time I laid eyes on my third ex-husband? I knew he was trouble. And sure enough."

"Amazing."

"That's not all. I can predict the future."

"I see."

"Ask me something big."

"How does the world end?"

"Not with a bang but a whimper."

Now I *was* amazed. "Clairvoyant *and* educated."

"Got a friend who's interested in the poetry. Ask me somethin' else. Somethin' closer to hand. Somethin' you really wanna know."

I nodded. "I really want to know what I'm having for dinner. Had a long drive on an empty stomach."

She whisked away my wine and walked toward the other end. Over her shoulder she answered, "That's easy. Scallops. They're very fresh." She put two bottles beside what looked like her own purse under the cash register. The other she turned, opened slowly, popped the cork, sniffed it, smiled, and poured me a taste.

She came back, set the glass—along with the cork—in front of me. I saluted her with the glass, and took the first sip. It's very rich, even right when you open it. "Well, okay. I love scallops, you know."

She closed her eyes. "Yes. I know. What kind of clairvoyant would I be?"

"Where are they, these scallops?"

"Down at the end of the beach, little shack." She shrugged. I had the idea I'd see it when I got there.

"How are they cooked?"

"Lightly sautéed. Ask for one of Tina's tables. She's my girl. What I don't know, she does."

"Okay. Tina's table."

"What else?"

I took another sip and looked around. The place was nearly empty. "Okay, what about the Turner boys?"

"Sorry?"

"Dally told you why I'm here."

She took a second, then decided to be straight with me. "Uh-huh, but they're not on Tybee, that I know—or they're really crafty."

"I'm told that's not an option." I sipped again. "But you never know."

"Cops don' think they're here. Police been an' gone; swarmed ever'-which where. Didn't find a trace. Boys're most likely in Savannah."

I set the glass down and gazed out the window at the blue, blue sky and the white ocean breaking. "So. Maybe I'm just here on vacation."

She was sympathetic to the idea. "It's nice here this time a year. What with the ocean an' everything."

I held out my hand. "How about telling my fortune? Am I going to have a good vacation?"

She glanced down at my hand. "You got a big surprise comin' to you."

"Really. And what might that be?"

"If I tell you," she patted the bar and strolled away, "it won't be a surprise."

I had to hound her. "That's easy for you to say. Anything remotely out of the ordinary after such a pronouncement, it's bound to seem like a fulfillment."

She didn't look back. "The world is fulla skeptics."

I had to agree. And by my reckoning, the world is also short on poetry-quoting barkeeps. She had, after all, foretold my scallops, which I was bound to have. So what did I have to lose? I had to ask the last question.

"What about a Lydia Habersham?"

She froze. "What about her?"

"She's been known to haunt these parts."

"So?"

"So is she here now?"

June came back to me with her attitude adjusted more than somewhat. "I kinda feel Lydia is like a second daughter to me, right? I don't want anything to happen to her."

I looked at my glass. "What could happen to her?"

"Guy like you? I'm guessing just about anything."

I sipped. So why was everybody so protective-feeling about Lydia? I decided on a change of approach. "How'd you come to know her?"

"She had a big boat out here, charter fishing mostly. Before she got married to that skunk. Came in here of an evening to listen to the tunes. Didn't drink, but liked the company. She's a livin' doll. I got attached right away."

I could tell there was more to it than that. I set the glass down again; couldn't help noticing she talked about Lydia in the past tense. "Big boat. She had dough."

June shook her head. "Parents give her money to keep away from 'em. They didn't care much for her, seemed to me. She's not like other girls."

Seemed to be the story I was getting from most everybody. "Got a picture?"

She blinked and then stared. I returned the favor. Finally she straightened and got a little framed newspaper article from off the wall behind her. It was a color feature article in the local paper all about a girl who'd been missing three weeks at sea with no provisions and came back into Tybee one afternoon fresh as a daisy like nothing had happened. She said she thought she'd been gone for a day or two. The picture wasn't much help. Lydia looked pale and thin, with long sun-blond hair flying every which way in the ocean breeze, covering up most of her face. Even so, I guess most anybody would have set her down as pretty. And there was even something vaguely familiar about her, like a fashion model, maybe. I wished I could have gotten a better look at her face.

I handed the frame back to June. "What happened? Where was she all that time?"

June put the thing back in its place of honor. "The explanations run from alien abduction to some Cuban drug connection."

"Which one do you buy?"

She shrugged. "Lydia loves the ocean. She just lost track of the time."

For three weeks? But I didn't say it. Instead: "So, are you going to guard my wine for me, or not?"

She was happy to return to less personal matters. "Like it was my own. You see, I set it right next to my purse."

"I noticed."

"By the way, you got a little trouble ahead of

you. You wanna be careful." She tapped her fore-head, right about the position of the third eye, if you believe that sort of thing.

"Must be a kind of curse, this psychic thing."

She glanced up at the wall clock. "Why doncha finish off that glass and take a little nap before dinner? You been travelin'."

Now, a nap is just fine with me nearly any time of the day, but I got the idea she knew something I didn't. Still, I felt she was full of good advice and kind intention, so I indulged her by tossing back the rest of the Simard and leaving a five on the bar beside my empty glass.

I stood up, but I couldn't resist the jukebox. I sidled over, idly pocketed a pack of matches from the top of it—never know when you're going to need a light. I checked the selections, popped a quarter in, and mashed R2: "Stardust." It was good exit music.

Up the stairs I could still hear it a little. I was humming to myself, when I noticed the door to my room was open. I stopped humming, walked slower. Maybe it was the maid service. I poked my head in. There was somebody in the suite all right. They were in the other bedroom; sounded like they were rummaging around. I slipped up to the doorframe and tried to get a peep in. All I could see was a smallish figure bent over one of the drawers looking for something.

I stepped into the doorway to block egress. "Looking in the wrong place, pal. My stuff's in the other bedroom. Something I could help you with?"

And who should turn around with the face of an

angel and a dress in each hand but none other than Dalliance Oglethorpe.

She smiled big. "Yeah, you can help me decide which one of these things to wear to go to dinner with you."

I must have been smiling pretty good too. "Well, you got me. This is indeed a surprise, as our psychic bartender downstairs just foretold."

"I've got to admit I put her up to it." She dropped the darker of the two dresses on the bed. "I tried to hint to you. When's the last time I closed Easy just because one of the utilities didn't work?"

I nodded. "Yeah, I thought that was a little fishy, if I may use that word on an island such as this."

"You may. How's June?"

"Cagey."

"We go way back."

"I gathered. She's pretty sure, by the way, that the boys aren't here."

"She ought to know, or her daughter, one or the other."

I leaned against the doorframe. "We'll ask to-night at dinner, I guess. She told me about some scallops on the other end of the island that her daughter will be only too glad to bring us."

"Tina? She's a good kid."

She held up the blue number in her left hand. I nodded. "I'm not sure exactly why you're here."

She went to hang it up on her bathroom door, yakking at me over her shoulder. "I've got news; plus, I want to hear what's up."

I retired to the sitting room that divided our two

bedrooms. The view of the beach was very absorbing. I couldn't take my eyes off it, even when Dally came in and sat beside me.

She stared too. "Great room, huh?"

"Nice window."

I took the next twenty minutes filling her in: meeting the folks in Tifton, Mr. Turner, the Peakers, the cop.

As it turned out, she'd been working too. "Called the Tifton Home Loan. They have, in fact, got a parent bank in Savannah: Southeastern Federal. What's the connection?"

"I have no idea."

"Why'd you want to know?"

"I'm telling you, I've got a hunch."

She wasn't impressed. "Uh-huh."

"Sling me that phone book beside you. Let's try a little something. You'll see. This hunch thing, it's a system with me. You absolutely *have* to follow your instincts. They tell you so much more than your noodle."

She rolled her eyes. "Anybody ever accuse you of bein' too much in touch with your feminine side?"

I squinted. "Nobody alive."

She grinned, reached over to the table by her elbow, and tossed me the Savannah Bell. I flipped to the *S*'s and dialed the front desk.

"Hello, Mr. Tucker."

"Hey. Could I get an outside line again, please?"

"Right away."

Dial tone. I popped in the number.

A woman answered. "Southeastern Federal."

"Hey, I got a Ms. Lydia Habersham here wants to

cash a check for a hundred dollars. Just making sure it's covered."

Pause.

"Who is this?"

"It's Tony over at the marina."

"Ms. Habersham has *loans* with us. We don't handle any checking. May I speak with her, please?"

"Uh . . . sure. Hang on."

I covered the phone tight with my hand and whispered to Dally, "She wants to talk to Lydia. You've got loans, but they don't do checking. Keep it terse, they might know her voice."

Dally gave me the eye, but she took the phone. I moved in close to listen. She spoke. "Hi."

"Ms. Habersham?"

"Uh-huh."

"Are you all right?"

"Uh-huh."

"You know you don't have checking with Southeastern Federal, darlin'."

"Oh. Is this Southeastern Federal? Shoot. I must have given him the wrong number."

Pause. "The wrong number?"

"Uh-huh."

"Who is this?"

I punched the button and the phone disconnected. Dally handed me back the receiver and I put the phone on the table.

I shook my head. "So she's got an account there."

She grinned. "That's part of *my* news."

"What?"

She was very pleased with herself. "*I've* got an account there too. Care to go check on it?"

"You put money into Southeastern Federal?"

She stood. "Had to. I wanted all my phone calls to carry weight. Money talks. Anyway, pays to spread it around. I diversify as much as you reminisce. Let's go into town. Maybe we can find out more."

Something was up with her. She was never *this* interested in the work she got me. Plus, what was she doing slinging her money around the state like that? I tried to hedge. "I was going to take a nap."

"Jeez, Flap. Show a little gumption. Savannah's only twenty minutes away the way I drive. We can make it right now if we hurry. Come on."

Five minutes later we were barreling down the road nearly a hundred miles an hour in Ms. Oglethorpe's red convertible rental job, headed for downtown Savannah. I tried to holler at her with the wind whipping around us.

"Things seem to be moving a little fast, doncha think?"

But she couldn't hear me. Probably wouldn't have agreed anyway.

15

Money and Marigolds

In Savannah the humidity was exactly 100 percent. You could literally swim through the air. The South-eastern Federal building was imposing, sunny, land-scaped within an inch of its life—but it was mostly marigolds, a pedestrian annual that I personally wouldn't give you the time of day for. I was happy to get out of the heat. Dally was happy to be in on the work. She didn't ordinarily tag along with me, but I had the sense she was especially interested in this one—plus, she was having fun. It was like a beach vacation for her, too, I guess—and who was I to spoil her vacation?

I nodded toward a loan officer in the row of desks to our left. "Get the younger guy there."

"What for?"

"Because we know for sure that *he's* not the per-son we talked to on the phone a minute ago. That was, if you'll recall, a woman. And because he'll find you enchanting. All the young guys do."

She accepted it, and we ambled toward him in a friendly enough fashion. He saw us coming and set down the papers he was reading.

"How are you?"

Dally smiled. I've already mentioned what kind of an effect that can have. "Fine and dandy. Just want to check on my account."

"Have a seat." He was very happy to help us.

We sat. She did the talking. "Dalliance Ogle-thorpe. Just transferred some funds here from Atlanta. Lookin' to add another nightclub to my chain."

He was very friendly. "Chain-chain-chain. Just like the song."

She nodded. "Exactly. I got a place in Atlanta called Easy, this'll be Easy Two."

"Easy To. Let's just have a look." He leaned forward and attacked his computer keyboard. Something impressive came up. His face was very clear on that.

Dally was cool. "So I want to buy up a place used to be called the Night Flight Cafe." She tossed me a look. God bless her.

The bank guy shook his head. He'd never heard of it.

"River Street."

He looked at his screen again. "You got enough here to buy and build anywhere you want to." He looked up. "How can I help?"

"Got some construction people over in Tifton, believe it or not, that are gonna give me a deal too good to pass up. You're associated with Tifton

Home Loan. I want to put some of the money there."

"Yes, ma'am. We're a parent company now, but I'll bet we could find some boys here in town that could give you just as good a deal."

"Free lumber, minimum-wage labor, no outside contractors. Also"—she dropped her voice, very conspiratorially—"all licenses for the work, including plumbing and electrical, are free."

He sat back, lowered his voice too. "Okay, you're right. We can't beat that." He was less enthusiastic than he had been a minute earlier. He was thinking: How does somebody get a deal like that? He was thinking: organized crime. It might as well have been written on his face. I tried to look tough, to support the illusion.

Dally forged on. "You don't know a guy there in Tifton by the name of Lowe Acree, do you?"

"Sure." But he was tight-lipped. Apparently knowing that this had something to do with Lowe Acree only confirmed his suspicions, because he had quit looking at his computer or making eye contact with either one of us. "Uh, Ms. Felton would probably be the one to help you with all this. She's our real estate expert and she's the one that works most closely with Mr. Acree."

After a second Dally had to ask. "Could you point her out?"

He tipped his head to the left and we saw Ms. Felton at her desk. I stood as much like a gangster as I could manage, hands folded in front of me. It was kind of fun, playing the hood. Dally smiled. We moved on.

As we were walking over, I whispered in Dally's ear, "Ten to one you've just had a recent phone conversation with this Ms. Felton."

She kept her eyes ahead, nodded. "No bet."

When we approached her, Ms. Felton smiled. I smiled back. It was like she'd been expecting us to come on over. Dally sat without being invited.

"How may I help you all?"

Dally spoke in a voice lower and slower than her normal musical tones. "Your cohort over there just told us you were the one to see about some real estate and some connecting funds in Tifton with a Lowe Acree."

"Oh." Ms. Felton was very small all of a sudden.

"Something wrong?"

She hesitated. "I don't know that I'm the one to tell you all this. Did you know Mr. Acree well?"

"Just on the phone."

"Well." She was a little relieved. "He's . . . passed on."

Dally was sympathetic. "Really. I'm sorry. Is Lydia all right?"

She brightened again. "Oh, you know Lydia?"

"Better than Lowe. I'm an Oglethorpe."

This seemed to make Ms. Felton very much more comfortable. "Oh. An Oglethorpe. I thought your voice sounded familiar. Are you close to the family here in Savannah?"

"Naw. I'm in Atlanta. Still, it's a shock: Lowe."

She agreed. "It's a shock." Ms. Felton lowered her voice. "They say somebody killed him."

Dally went into mother mode. "Oh, Lydia must

be beside herself. Is she out there at the house, do you know?"

Ms. Felton nodded, but she didn't make eye contact. "I believe she'd probably be at home, but I don't really know."

Dally looked out the window. "How do I get there from here, I'm all turned around. It's, what— north on . . ."

Ms. Felton nodded again. ". . . Main till you get to Peoples, then, you know, right on Habersham."

"That's right. Well." She stood. "I'm Dalliance, and this is my associate, Mr. Tucker. He may be following up for me on the real estate and money details, but I think I need to see if Lydia's all right before I can concentrate on anything else. You understand."

She understood. "You go right ahead. I'll . . . check with Jimmy." And she gave the guy we'd just spoken to a little look. What she'd check I had no idea.

We waved good-bye and were out the door so quick that the heat of the day took my breath away. "Well, that was weird. And, if I may say so, that's some pretty good bluffing for an amateur."

She patted my arm. "Not really a bluff. For one thing, the rich *always* live north."

"Still—must have been a pretty impressive amount in the account to make young Jimmy that nervous. I think he felt you were connected."

She shrugged. "Money talks."

"No it doesn't. It just bullies people around."

She wasn't buying. "Whatever. It gets the job done."

"But it's rude."

"What do you care?"

I opened her car door for her. "I'm polite. I
don't like to see any sort of rude behavior. It wor-
ries me."

16

Impatiens

We headed in a northerly direction. I didn't remotely expect to find Lydia at home in her palatial estate, but Dally loves to look over the playpens of the idle rich. Habersham Drive was no trouble to find; Number One Habersham was even easier: had a big sign in Deco lettering over the gate.

We turned in; up the long, tree-lined drive. A guy in very nice casual dress, with a drink in his hand, met us outside the front door. Before the motor was off, he was sticking his other hand in to shake with Dally.

"You must be Dalliance Oglethorpe."

Dally was cordial enough. "I must be. This is my associate, Flap Tucker."

The casual guy was very glad to meet me too. "Ms. Felton phoned to say you were on your way. We've been worried sick about Lydia."

I got out of the passenger side without any help from the casual guy, but Dally wasn't so lucky. He was all over her: opening her door, squiring her elbow, all manner of very Southern Gentlemanly Behavior. It was okay by me, but she felt a little hemmed in by it, I could tell.

I spoke up. "Ms. Felton just called you?"

He waved his drink a little carelessly. "To let us know you were on the way."

Dally took a polite step away from him. "So is she in? Lydia?"

The casual guy seemed confused. "In? What do you mean . . . here?" He blinked like he was trying to understand another language. "No." He took a quick glance to the house. "We thought *you* knew where she was. Aren't you the detectives from Atlanta?"

So much for any further bluffing. I piped up again. "I'm a licensed private investigator. Ms. Oglethorpe is a businessperson. She's a proprietress."

He was still confused. "You mean that rigamarol about a new nightclub on River Street—that's true?"

She nodded. "You bet."

"And you don't know where Lydia is?"

"Nope."

He was getting funnier. "And you actually thought she was here?"

I had to chime in. "Could we take all this from the top? We didn't think she was here, but we've got to check everything. Plus, we could use a little information from the parents."

It took him a second, but he relaxed. "Of course. Would you come in?"

The house was big and white and old, with a staircase in the entrance room big enough for Rhett to ride a brace of Tennessee Walkers up and down all day long. Everything looked like it was meant as a set piece, not a real thing. That's the way a lot of rich people like it: like nobody really lived there.

The place was also lousy with portraiture, mostly relatives, by the titles, but without a trace of family resemblance to one another. I took a shine to one just above the staircase underpass. It was of a young, blond, winsome woman, once again vaguely familiar; as far as I could tell something roughly like the face I'd seen in the newspaper photo at June's bar.

I took a shot. "That's Lydia?"

The casual guy had to look to make sure. "No. It's an antique, but it *does* look like her, doesn't it? Quite the belle. I think it was painted by Winslow Homer."

I wasn't impressed. "Homer didn't do portraits."

He misunderstood. "I'm not that fond of it either."

We followed him into the kitchen. There was a woman around his age sitting at the breakfast table. She was in a crisp striped shirt and white, white slacks. The room looked out some pretty impressive French doors that opened onto a patio, and the outside was wild with impatiens. Now there's a flower: grows in the shade; blooms like crazy; reseeds itself if you let it, and the winter's not too rough.

I couldn't resist. "Nice spread of impatiens."

She didn't even look. "All volunteers. We think they were planted at the turn of the century originally." They were huge, mostly purple.

The casual guy was a little less than patient himself. "This is my wife, Eugenia."

I nodded. "Flap Tucker."

She nodded right back. "Where's Lydia?"

I liked that: right to the point. "Do you think she might be on Tybee?"

They didn't agree, I could tell. Eugenia was very clear. "She wouldn't go back there."

Her husband was still interested, at least. "What makes you think that she's there?"

I shrugged. "A hunch."

He looked at his wife. "But they also thought she might be *here*."

The wife got a laugh out of that. "So you don't really know anything?"

I looked at the tabletop. "May I sit?"

She tossed her right hand; I took it as assent, and grabbed a chair. "Ms. Habersham, I've been doing this kind of work for a great many years now. I don't feel a need to tell you my life story, but I know what I'm doing. Whenever I look for something, I find it. It's just that simple. Right now I'm only looking for your daughter in order to find some other people. When, and I say *when* I find her, she may want to get lost again. Happens that way sometimes. If she killed her husband, that's neither here nor there to me. All I'm asked to do is find two boys from Beautiful. They're here in Savannah, or out on Tybee, because of your daughter. They want to help her. Once I find the boys, I tell their daddy where they are. Then I'm done. So I'm only looking for Lydia because she's hooked up with the Turner twins. Okay?"

That was end of my speech. It seemed to make Mrs. Habersham feel better, somehow. But the Mister was a little different. He wanted more.

"If you find Lydia, you'll bring her to us."

I looked out at the impatiens. "Not if she doesn't care to come."

He set his drink down on the table a little louder than he needed to. "I'm not suggesting that she'd have an option."

Dally stepped in. "We thought we were bein' pretty cool with everybody. How'd you know we were 'the detectives from Atlanta'?"

Mr. Habersham didn't look at Dally, but he finally answered her. "Ms. Felton and . . ."

Mrs. Habersham filled in. ". . . Jimmy . . ."

He went on. ". . . from the bank . . . they're not as stupid as you might think. And they have Caller ID. They knew the supposed call from Lydia and somebody at the marina had actually come from the DeSoto. They just called back and checked your room and found out your names. They were also a little suspicious about Ms. Oglethorpe's . . . business plan." He finally looked at her. "You're not really going to build a new nightclub on River Street."

Dally just smiled. "It'll be done by Christmas . . . St. Patrick's Day at the latest." She can be as tough as she wants to be.

He turned back to me. "Then there was the earlier call from June over at the DeSoto Lounge. She's a great friend of Lydia's. She wanted to let us know that Mr. Tucker was on the job. She doesn't care for us much. She wanted us to know she knew more about our daughter than we did. She thinks you'll find her— I don't know why." He gathered his thoughts, I was pretty sure he'd been drinking all day. "I think that brings us up to date, more or less. Now, shall we discuss the terms of your employment?"

I adjusted my chair. "I already have a client. Not to mention that the police in Tifton feel I'm already getting in their way. I can't do what ten people tell me to do."

Dally amplified. "In the words of the immortal Otis Redding."

I nodded. "So, thank you for your generous offer, and perhaps we could work together in the future sometime, but I regret that, for the moment, I must take a pass on your current offer of employment."

Mrs. Habersham sank. "You won't help us?"

Mr. Habersham steeled. "He's just bargaining. He wants money."

I had to disagree. "I've got everything I could ever want. It's not the money. Mr. Turner over in Beautiful seems like a great guy, and I want to help. Anyway"—I looked at Dally—"I only take work if *Ms. Oglethorpe* asks me to."

He snapped his eyes on Dally. "So you're the business manager."

She was growing impatient. It seemed to be a theme. "Look, I've got a list of people I'm keepin' informed about Mr. Tucker's progress in this matter. You want to be on the list, it won't cost a dime—unless it's a long-distance call, then I'll reverse the charges. Otherwise I'll let you know just like everybody else. It's a courtesy. Mr. Tucker is very big on courtesy—aren't you, Flap."

"Yes, ma'am." I smiled.

This only seemed to make Mr. Habersham madder. "You look here—"

I interrupted. "You're worried about your little girl. If it's any consolation, everybody I've met so far seems to feel the same way. Can you see that Mr. Turner is worried about his sons the same way? Not to mention Tommy the policeman, who's worried about his cousin that got dead. Everybody's worried about family—everybody but me. I don't really think about my family all that much—with the possible exception of a bizarre array of unfortunates who inhabit Ms. Oglethorpe's joint in Atlanta. So excuse me if I don't quite *get* the family thing. All I'm out to do is find two boys. If, in the course of human events, I find your daughter by and by, I'll let her know you're worried. How about that? Then, if she feels like it, Ms. Oglethorpe will be in touch. That's as good as it's going to get." I stood, mostly for punctuation.

He couldn't decide whether to keep his mad on or go with the situation. His wife helped. She was very quiet. "Thank you, Mr. Tucker. We'd appreciate that."

Manners do count for something. Mr. Habersham looked down. "Mr. Tucker, we've not always been the perfect parents. We're not currently the perfect parents." He picked up his drink again. I'd decided it was scotch. "We'll never be the perfect parents. Not for her. Lydia is a very strange girl."

The Missus was worried about it, too, but she tried to make light. "We often imagine she was exchanged at birth for a human child."

No one took it as the joke she'd meant it to be.

Dally couldn't resist. "She's a creature of the sea."

Mr. Habersham resumed. "As a child in Charleston she was always at the beach. She didn't care about school or boys or clubs or anything important.

She couldn't do anything right. When she was old enough, she was always out on the ocean. She never wanted our help. She always earned her own way. After she took up that *job,* we hardly saw her." Sip. He'd said *job* like it was a communicable disease. "We shouldn't have let her marry."

The mother picked up. "She met that Lowe Acree and he was the first man who went out of his way to be nice to her, and it turned her head—turned our heads, too, I suppose. She married him in one big whirl."

Dally couldn't resist. "Marry in haste, repent in leisure."

The Mister ignored it. "She's not like other people. She's like a little fragile doll." He took a sip and looked at the impatiens. "And she didn't kill anyone, by the way. She's not capable."

In a lot of fathers that assessment would have come off like a compliment to their little girls. This one sounded like an indictment. Like it was just one more thing his kid couldn't do right.

Mrs. Habersham wound things up for us. "So— thank you again for your offer. We'd like very much to be kept informed."

Informed seemed to me a cold word for the situation. But I guess this *is* the Information Age.

Dally shot out her hand to the man. "Then you'll be hearing from me soon."

And that was it. Our little visit to Tara was finished. Mr. Habersham showed us to the door. He didn't say good-bye.

As we were pulling out the gate, I looked back

over my shoulder at the huge house. "They don't seem all that much like parents, do they?"

"How would you know?"

"They didn't seem odd to you?"

"A little, but how do you mean?"

"More like . . . keepers than parents."

She shrugged. "Lots of parents seem like jailers, especially to their children—don't they?"

I turned back forward again; shrugged. "Maybe you're right. How would I know what lots of parents are supposed to seem like?"

I was thinking about my grandmother filling up a shopping cart with forty-three boxes of Bon Ami.

17

Frim Fram Sauce

We were back on Tybee and, well within the hour, walking down the beach toward our dinner. We were practically alone on the beach, except for a fat tourist in a white tank top and black shorts wading in the waves behind us.

Dally was examining my intuitions. "So what's your hunch here, pal?"

I was happy to supply. "For no good reason, I got the idea there's some *one* thing that makes all this go around. Could it have something to do with drugs?"

"What?" She stopped walking. "You think all this has something to do with drugs?"

"I know it's a cliché."

"Worse. It's a mundane cliché."

"I can't help it. I've had this hunch since I left Atlanta."

"How come?"

"I had a brief talk with our local pharmaceutical distributor."

"The guy that interrupted my swordfish?"

I nodded. "That's the guy."

She was skeptical. "There's got to be more to your hunch than *that*."

I kept right on. "Well, there were the jumpy kids that popped me on the highway."

"The bold, hick highwaymen."

"Uh-huh, and one of them seemed *very* hopped up on bennies."

She had to laugh. "*Hopped up on bennies?* In what decade?"

I ignored. "Then there was the dead banker who wanted Turner land for a *chemical* dump—"

"Hold it. What?"

"Did I forget to mention that?"

She looked away. "Chemical dump."

I went on. "Then, Lydia was missing for days and nobody knew why, and one of the theories floating around town about that was some sort of Cuban drug connection."

"Where'd you get *that*?"

"From June, your turncoat friend."

"She's not a turncoat, she's got dual citizenship."

"What?"

"She's loyal to more than one flag at a time. She's my pal, but she obviously has some feeling for Lydia."

"At least."

"So what's the drug deal?"

"I don't know. But Horace, that's the guy with the curbside drugstore outside my window, he told me about the new thrill."

"Which is?"

"A little concoction known as Homicide: skag, coke, *and,* get this, some kind of seasickness medication."

She squinted. "I think I heard something about it on the news. S'posed to make you really nuts; violent."

"There you are."

"So you're implying that Lowe Acree . . ."

". . . and, you know, maybe even his cousin Tommy . . ."

She stopped again. ". . . the cop?"

"Right."

"You're saying they wanted the Turner land in order to dump *those* chemicals?"

I shook my head. "Well, I don't know. Maybe they don't want to dump anything. Maybe they just wanted privacy for whatever it is they *were* doing. When you mention the phrase *chemical dump,* most people are going to stay far away. I get the impression that the land's pretty secluded anyway—so whatever goes on out there can stay a secret as long as it wants to."

"And how exactly is Lydia involved in this bizarre scenario you've invented?"

"I didn't invent it—I intuited it." But my shoulders sagged. "Though it doesn't really seem all that likely, does it?"

"Not really."

"Not really."

She thought on. "Could it have something to do with the bank connections? I don't know . . . money laundering?" She looked out to sea again. "Or what if it's something else—something really weird? Like this Lydia really is something out of this world."

I shrugged. "You can get that feeling, but it's just that everybody tries to keep this odd envelope of protection around her. She's the connection between all the players, *that's* the truth. So maybe she *is* that one thing that I'm looking for."

Dally nodded. "You're always telling me that the simplest answer is the best."

I nodded slowly. "Most of the time."

"So maybe it's just as simple as this: She *did* kill her husband, she's nuts, and everybody's just watching out for her because she can't do it herself. You're so paranoid sometimes, you think there's some sort of bigger conspiracy behind everything. Maybe this is just a small-town murder and a perfectly acceptable brand of Southern madness."

It was all sand castles. When you dope out a situation like this, pardon the expression, you have to be prone to wild speculation for a while. It helps to define the parameters. In point of fact we had no idea what we were talking about. So we walked a little way then without gabbing.

The old paranoia nerve *was* acting up on me, though—maybe because Dally'd brought it up. The guy in black trunks and a white tank top had been walking with us a little too long for coincidence, in my book. By the time we were at the other end of the island, I started to turn around and ask him a few choice questions, but then he just walked on by us like we weren't even there.

I relaxed, and then my stomach started asking all kinds of questions about dinner.

I was peering into the clump of buildings. "Which one is the restaurant?"

Dally just headed in. "Smell."

I did, but once you're at the ocean, it all smells like that to me.

She followed her nose, and before I could object, we were at the door of The Hut.

I guess we were a little early for dinner. The place was nearly empty. A sandy-headed kid took us right to a booth that looked out at the ocean.

I didn't sit. "We have to be in Tina's station."

The kid smiled. "I know. June called. Made a reservation in y'all's name. Tucker, right?"

Dally nodded. "How'd you know it was us?"

She eyeballed me. "She said watch out for a man to come up from the beach in a suit an' tie. I took a shot."

We sat. The booth was cozy. Before we could even take in the view, Tina was at our side.

"Hey. Momma said ya'll'd be here 'bout now. Already got you some scallops cookin'. How 'bout a salad or an appetizer?"

Dally sighed. "I'd better get some cold shrimp."

She agreed. "I think you better."

I was more trouble. "What are the appetizers?"

She was easy. "Got just whatcha want. It's some little fillets of shark wrapped around some smoked mussels; lightly sautéed in a basil champagne. Five or six on the plate. It'll kill you."

I smiled. "I may never get another chance to be killed by a shark. I'm not much of a swimmer."

She nodded, humoring me. "Well, then." And she was gone like a shot.

Then, before I could even worry about what to drink, Tina was back with two glasses of red wine.

She set them on the table like they were the crown jewels.

"I know you said you didn't want nobody else drinkin' this stuff, but Momma figured you wouldn't mind sharin' with Ms. Oglethorpe."

I couldn't believe it. "This is my Simard?"

"Uh, it's your red wine, yes, sir. Momma sent it over. Is that all right?"

I took a sip. It was indeed my stuff. "This may be the best service I've ever had at a seafood joint anywhere in the world."

She smiled. "I thought it was white wine was for fish."

I set her straight. "*Wine* is only red . . . and French. Everything else is just deluding itself."

"Okay." She winked. Some waitresses can pull it off. She was one. "I'll check on your appetizers." And she was gone.

Dally appreciated the wine. "Is this the '83?"

"Your palate's getting better."

"The '86 is good, but it's not this . . ."

". . . polished . . ."

". . . or somethin'."

I sat back. "I'm happy."

She set her glass down and looked out the window. "So, let me get right to the point: Do you just *think* the boys are here because that's what some people are telling us, or did you do your thing?"

She never liked to talk about it, even though it was the basis for the work she got me. I have a gift. I got it when I was a kid. Some kids can sing, and some can play ball; some turn to petty crime or drugs if they have a talent for that sort of thing. Me, I've got a trick. It's one of the reasons I'm so good at what I do. In short here's the deal: You sit quiet enough for long enough and breathe the right way and don't disturb the images that come to you—a little like trying to catch a big bass in a small pond—and then you can see everything. I mean everything in the universe that you want to know. First you see a kind of golden curtain, and sometimes the images play in front of it, like a performance, like the play in God's mind. If you can leave them alone, they tell you everything. Maybe I'm not explaining it well. I see the whole of the thing, like pieces of a puzzle, and the puzzle drops into place; I know where the missing thing is, and I can find it. I did it first when I was just a kid, looking for something important to Dally. She lost a ring that meant something to her, and I found it. After that I knew I could do it every time. It's not a substitute for getting out in the great wide world and asking the right questions and seeing the wrong people. It's in the middle of everything else. That doesn't really explain anything, I know. If I could say it in any better words, it still wouldn't be the real thing anyway. You can't communicate this kind of thing in words.

I think that's what shakes Dally up the most about it. She really loves to talk, and I don't talk about it all that much. It makes most people nervous. Even makes some want to shove me in the nuthouse. But I'm not nuts. Ask anybody. All *I* am is quirky.

So I kept my answer short. "Nope. Haven't yet."

We were rescued from further exploration of the subject by the swift and certain delivery of our appetizers.

Tina was very proud. "Best seafood on the East Coast, right here." And she slid the plates in front of us.

Mine was like a little work of modern art: the tight cuts of rolled fillet arranged around the parsley and mussels in the middle, festive chives everywhere. Dally had a glass cup of mammoth cold shrimp still in their shells and another champagne glass filled with red sauce.

Tina beamed. "I'll just get you all some bread."

Dally piped up. "Maybe a bottle of spring water?"

"Quebelle?"

"Fine."

She shot away.

Dally popped open one of her prizes and dipped it up to her fingers in the sauce. I tried to keep up with her, and swirled one of my little morsels in the sauce on the plate and popped it into my mouth.

She reacted. "Jeez. This sauce is *hot*. Must be the horseradish. But man, these shrimps are fresh. How's yours?"

"Great. A little sweeter than I thought it would be. I guess it's the champagne sauce. Frim fram sauce."

She squinted, like she couldn't concentrate. "What?"

I was a little vague too. " 'Frim Fram Sauce'—it was the song on the B-side of Nat 'King' Cole's single of 'Route 66.' Makes the shark more like a kind of coquilles Saint Jacques kind of thing. The sauce is really . . . strong."

I took one more bite; Dally scooped up another dollop of hot sauce with a shrimp—and we were both unconscious in the next split second, like a ton of bricks, like babies falling asleep. Out like lights. Blink. The old seafood mickey. And that's when the real strangeness began.

10

A Wide, Wide Sea

When I woke up, I felt like I'd been run over by a team of Clydesdales—and the beer wagon they'd been dragging behind them. There was the sensation that somebody was jabbing a golden spear into my eyes, but it turned out to be the sun through the blinds. I was in a little room smaller than my galley kitchen back home, on a cot that folded down from the wall. It took me a minute to realize it wasn't me that was dizzy, it was the room.

The room was pitching up and down. I only had to concentrate another five minutes or so to realize this had something to do with the fact that I was on a boat.

I tried to get my bearings. I shook my head. On the little table beside me there was an old book, *Lamb's Tales from Shakespeare*—I used to have one just like it when I was a kid. I started to pick it up. Then there was a rumble of thunder outside, or maybe it was in my head. This was some unbelievable drug hangover.

Just as I was trying to get up off the bunk, somebody came into the room.

"Hey. You 'wake?"

I wasn't sure. "Maybe."

"How you feel?"

"How long have I been out?"

"All night."

"What time is it?"

"After noon."

My eyes focused. On the cot across from me was a big boy in his late twenties. He was plain and smiling; seemed familiar.

He patted my leg. "You'll be okay."

I withheld my judgment. "What happened?"

"Whatcha mean?"

"I mean how come I'm on a boat with you instead of at dinner with . . . where's Dally?"

"That lady you's with?"

I lurched up. He stiff-armed me in the sternum, knocked the breath out of me. It was casual. He meant no harm. I sat back. I was in no shape to go a round with this guy. I nodded. "Yeah, the lady. Where is she?"

"Back at her hotel room. She's fine. Prob'ly just gettin' up too."

"What'd you use to knock us out?"

"On you? Bovine tranquilizer."

I felt like it. "You didn't use this stuff on Dally?"

He grinned. "Naw. We just used some sleepin' pills on her. Daddy gets to where he can't sleep so good? And the doctor give 'im some pills. We let her have five and some alcohol. She be just fine, really. And we didn't give you all that much of the tranquilizer either. Me an' Peachy both taken it once, just to see what it was like." He crossed his legs and looked right at me. "If you jus' take a little? It's very relaxing."

I tried to focus my eyes. "I'm a little too relaxed right at the moment."

"It'll wear off. Wanna go swimmin'? That helps."

"We're on a boat, right?"

"Yup."

"Where?"

"On the ocean."

"Right. Where?"

He looked toward the window. "I don't know, exactly. Honest."

I sat up and really tried to get some eye contact. "So you've got to be Maytag Turner."

He was very happy about it. "Yup."

"Where'd you get a name like that?"

"Aunt Ida said when I was born, I was big as a warshin' machine."

"And your brother?"

"Not as big."

"No, I mean—how'd he get 'Peachy'?"

He rolled his head. "Ohhhh. He was second? And when he come out, Ida asked Momma was he as much trouble as I was? She said no, he was just peachy."

"It's a good story." A little lighthearted considering it might have been the last words their mother spoke.

He was willing to play along. "How 'bout 'Flap'? That's a name."

I dropped the chitchat. "You know my name. You knew where to find me to knock me out. What's the story?"

"We know all about you. Daddy told us you was comin'. We called him yesterday."

"So your daddy knows where you are?"

"Not exactly. But he knows we're okay. We don't really like to worry him."

I nodded. "He seemed kind of sickly."

The kid got serious. "He's been thataway since I can remember."

"Farming. It's hard work."

He agreed. Then he brightened again. "Wanna go up on top?"

"Uh-huh." I shoved myself up from the cot and he caught my arm. We navigated up the little stairs together.

On deck the light was so blinding, even though the sky was overcast and looked like it could rain any second, I had to close my eyes completely. Somebody plopped a cap on my head and put some sunglasses in my hand. I must have looked pretty silly in my rumpled suit and my John Deere cap, but I didn't care. Even with the cap and the Ray-Bans, I could barely see.

When my pupils finally closed a little, I could tell there was another kid at the rail with a big deep-sea fishing pole in his hands.

He craned backward. "Hey, Mr. Tucker. How's you head?"

I waved. Pays to be friendly. "Feels like a cow."

He laughed. Maytag brought me something to drink, a Coke, maybe, and I sat down on one of the hatches. The boat wasn't huge, but big enough to handle six people very comfortably. It looked like any other charter fishing boat.

Maytag called out to his brother. "Catchin' anything?"

"Naw."

"Then come have a little talk with Mr. Tucker."

He set his pole in a lock at the top of the rail in front of him, and clomped over to us.

He threw his hand at me. "Peachy Turner."

I shook his hand. "That would have been my guess."

He sat. "Daddy hired you to find us?"

"Uh-huh. Looks like I earned my dough. Here you are."

They both thought that was pretty funny. I was wishing I had a way to check on Dally, see if she was okay. They must have seen something in my face.

Maytag shook his head. "We got nothin' against you, Mr. Tucker. We just wanted to . . . talk."

"Then how come the mickey in the seafood? How'd you do it, by the way?"

Maytag volunteered. "The bovine tranquilizer's a liquid, went into your sauce real easy. Not much taste, but it's a little sweet."

"I noticed."

"Uh-huh. Daddy's sleepin' pills is real bitter, though. So we had to spice up the lady's sauce pretty good."

I looked out to sea. No land anywhere. "Tina was in on it?"

Peachy nodded. "Tina and June both."

"Why?" At the moment that's all I wanted to know.

Maytag settled back and folded his arms in front of him. "Lydia."

I waited for more, but there was none. It was as if he'd made an eloquent speech. He was satisfied with it. I had to have more. "What about her?"

Peachy put his hand over his mouth, just like a grammar school kid thinking of the answer to a math problem. Then: "Lydia is not like anybody else in this world. We've been knowing her for a good while on Tybee. When you meet 'er? It's like meetin' a wild creature or a angel or a . . ." But he was at the end of his field of reference.

Maytag had to take over. "She don't talk like nobody else, she don't move like nobody else. She ain't"—he leaned in and lowered his voice—"we don't think she's human."

I was clearly skeptical. "Uh-huh. So you like her."

This gave them a laugh. Peachy made it clear. "Everybody likes her. Why you think you're here with us now? Nobody meets 'er that don't like 'er."

I pulled back. "Except her husband."

That got things quiet. It took a minute for May-tag to form his words. "Lowe Acree . . . is one of those men—and I'd say there's a lots of 'em now days, but Lowe's one of the worst—that's bent on wreckin' up the world. He wanted money and stuff and he didn't give a damn how he got it. Lydia was just somethin' else in his treasure chest."

Peachy was on fire with this idea now. "Like you

hear there's a lotsa rich men that buys up old pitch-
ers and pays a million dollars for 'em and they don't
really care to look at 'em or nothin'? It's just a investment to them. Beautiful paintin's they never even
look at." The way he said *investment* seemed to me
the closest Peachy Turner ever got to cursing.

Maytag helped me out. "We went to the High
Museum in Atlanta on a school trip once? They got a
lot of paintin's there."

Off in the distance, there was a little more thunder, and the sky was getting darker.

Peachy squinted hard. "If Lowe Acree had one of
those pretty things? He'd just put it in a vault some-
wheres, never look at it, never let nobody else look at
it, just see how much could he get for it. That's not
good."

I was sympathetic. "Plus, he wanted some land of
yours."

Maytag spit. "He didn't want no land. He wanted
a place to dump poison. He wanted a garbage can.
We don't own one a them." Then he grinned at his
brother.

I ignored it. "So you wouldn't sell."

Peachy smiled, back to his friendly self. "Not
really, no."

I pressed. "And he got all bent outta shape."

Maytag nodded. "He got right mad about it."

"And you all had an argument in his office and it
got outta hand."

Peachy smiled even bigger. "He called us retarded."

I nodded. "And it made you mad right back at
him."

Maytag shook his head slowly, surprised. "Lotsa

people calls us retarded. They don't mean nothin' by it."

Peachy filled me in. "We're not retarded."

Maytag agreed. "We're just simple."

Peachy sat back. "It's a gift to be simple."

Maytag patted his brother's leg. "It's the secret a life."

Peachy agreed. "Life is very easy, Mr. Tucker. Most people don't realize it, but it is."

Maytag looked out on the water, then at me. "Life is nothin' more or less than a little bubble on th' ocean. It comes up, it gets some sun on it, then it pops and goes back in the sea. That's all there is to it."

Peachy shook his head, sorry for everybody alive but himself and his kin. "So why in the world does everybody want to get so riled up about it?"

And for a second everything was still and calm on the ocean and in the air, the sun came out hard from behind a cloud, and I saw the world through their eyes. I'd have to say it was a place I could have lived, but the moment passed. Then, before I could pursue my line of thinking about the death of one Lowe Acree, there was a big splash near the boat.

Maytag jumped up. "We got somethin'!"

He ran to the rail, reared back on his pole at nearly a forty-five-degree angle from the deck. Peachy sat with me, smiling at his brother.

I straightened my hat. "Thanks for the brim."

He nodded. "Gotta keep the sun off."

"Peachy?"

"Uh-huh."

"Why am I here?"

He turned to me, very serious. "You gotta help us. We can't find Lydia and we're worried just sick about her. She's a very strange person and a lot of people don't understand her the way we do. We didn't see no need in your wastin' time lookin' for us: we're right here. So now all you gotta do is find Lydia. Okay?"

He returned his attention to his brother. Maytag was making fair progress collecting fishing line on his reel. Something big was at the other end. In spite of myself, and my desire to know what was what, I had to go see.

I lumbered up, and shoved myself over to the rail. The line was straight and tight, right into the sea. After a second the fish jumped up.

"Swordfish!" Peachy was beside himself. "Man-oh-man, I *love* me some swordfish."

Maytag looked over at me, very calmly under the circumstances. "It's great on the grill."

After another twenty or thirty minutes, there was a swordfish on the deck of our boat. Peachy popped a hatch and we all slid the thing down into a huge refrigerated hold. We were all pretty happy with ourselves, it had taken all three of us to get the thing in. I thought it was about a hundred and twenty feet long, but maybe I overestimated a little.

The boys popped open some beers, and then, without the slightest ceremony, reached into the cooler and slipped out a freezing, opened bottle of the Château Simard.

Maytag handed it over, with a plastic cup. "You had this at Tina's. She said you'd want it. I guess it was already paid for. We tried to get it nice an' cold for you."

True enough, there was ice on the bottle. I smiled. Their intentions were so good, I decided to spare them my usual wine rant. "Thanks."

Peachy was very happy. "Drink up."

I popped the cork, poured a full plastic cup, and we all toasted our catch. I had to get back to what I thought was really important. "I'm worried about Dally."

They nodded. Maytag patted my arm. "Wanna call 'er? We got a phone."

I must have lurched. I nearly spilled some of my stuff. "Yeah, I wanna call 'er."

Peachy disappeared below and came back ten seconds later with a cell phone. He handed it right to me. "Mash the code on the front first, then the motel."

I looked out to sea. "Don't know the motel number."

Maytag slugged back his beer. "Check the right coat pocket there, Mr. Turner. I believe you got some matches from the lounge." He looked down. "Sorry. We had to check your pockets."

Check for *what* we didn't get into. I looked; there they were: DeSoto Beach Motel Lounge matches. I dialed.

The desk answered. "DeSoto Beach Motel."

"Would you mind giving me Room Twenty-seven, please?"

"Surely."

There was a long series of ringing noises before she answered. "Uh-huh."

"Dally?"

She was immediately more alert. "Flap? Where are you?"

"On a boat out at sea—with the Turner twins."

"What?"

I shifted ears. "Yeah. How do you like that?"

"Not much, right at the moment. Are you okay?"

"Oh, yeah. I'm recovering from an overdose of bovine tranquilizer."

She still wasn't quite awake. "What happened to us?"

"We got slipped a mickey, as they say in the movies."

"Cow tranquilizer?"

"That's what I got. You got sleeping pills."

"Lucky me."

"Indeed."

"I kinda remember you goin' out before me . . . but I couldn't . . ." She yawned. "Did you say you're with the Turner twins?"

"Yup. They're the ones who popped us."

"Why?"

I looked at them. They were watching me, smiling. "I don't know. They say they want me to help 'em find Lydia."

"Oh." There was a rustling of sheets, like she was sitting up. "Flap?" There was a long pause. She was thinking, trying to clear her head. "There's something more about this deal that I didn't tell you because I wasn't sure about it, and I didn't know whether you'd wanna help, given that I know how you feel about family stuff and all, and it's not *just* Sally and Dally and J. D. Turner and the magnificent tapping aunt and the twins who don't look like twins . . ."

She was talking wacky. "Sugar, you're not awake yet."

"I know, but I gotta try an' tell you what's goin' on."

I could be patient. "Okay, tell me."

But she didn't get a chance. There was a crack of lightning, and more thunder, and the sky got darker all of a sudden, and the phone went dead.

I looked at the thing. "Damn."

Peachy looked around. "Lost your connection. It's a storm comin' up good. We best get on in."

Both boys got up and went to work. I tried a couple of times to redial, but there was nothing but static.

19

Bleak House

The rain came. The boys seemed to know what to do, and there wasn't much I had to offer in the way of help. So I let nature take its course. Its course seemed to take me where it wanted me to go anyway. That's a little lesson in the great Tao. I can't remember who said it, but the quote is, "Destiny leads those who will follow—and drags those who will not."

Whoever said it, I got the point: You're going whether you want to or not. You can walk along your path pleasantly enough, or you can go kicking and screaming. Either way, you'll end up in the same place when the day is done.

Anyway that's the way my thoughts were going when we pulled into a little dock under the black afternoon sky. There was nothing there but the dock and a path that curved into invisibility in the woods.

Peachy was tying up. "I believe that cold storage'll keep my fish all right. Reckon?"

I looked at him. "I dunno."

Maytag stepped onto the dock. "Whose fish, now?"

Peachy hopped. "You comin', Mr. Tucker?"

They both stood still, waiting for me to move. Was it just a bizarre trick of the light, or did these two look more like Pevus Arnold and Ronnie Tibadeau than they had out on the ocean? Whatever. Everybody's related to everybody else one way or the other.

I skipped off the boat. They both turned and headed up the path. I guess if I'd had the gumption, I could have zipped back on board, cast off, and set the boat west, hoping to bump into Georgia. I figured we were on Ossabaw or Cumberland or some smaller island off the coast. I couldn't help but hit the continent if I just headed west.

But the boys were my object. They were the prize. I was getting paid to find them—didn't seem right to try hard to lose them now. So I pulled my coat collar up around my neck to keep the rain out—and followed along the path.

After about five minutes or so we came to a very nice little house. It was all glass and exposed beams, a post–Frank Lloyd Wright job from the fifties or so. It was built right into the nature all around it, the kind of shack that probably had a name like Mandalay or Bleak House.

"Keen digs."

Peachy turned around. "Hmm?"

"I like the house."

"Oh. It don't belong to us."

Maytag was more helpful. "It's one that belongs to the Habershams or somebody else rich, and Lydia stayed here awhile. We thought we might find her here. It's where she'd usually come. But she ain't." He was doing his best to explain. "Here, I mean."

Peachy was opening up the front door. It wasn't locked. "This is where we called Daddy from first, but we didn't talk long."

Maytag nodded. "We seen that TV show where they trace the calls."

I nodded. "Yeah. I love that show." I had no idea what he was talking about.

We were in a neat living area with a stone fireplace and studied folk antiques. Maytag patted my shoulder and talked to me like I was a kid. "You hungry?"

I hadn't thought about it. "As a matter of fact."

He headed for the kitchen. You could see it around the edge of the hearth. "I believe we got some barbecue left. You like barbecue?"

"By the fifth or by the rib?"

He was baffled. "We just got sammiches."

I plopped down in a heavy overstuffed chair. "Okay."

Peachy came over to me. "You're kinda tired."

"Uh-huh."

"Takes awhile for the stuff to wear off." He patted my shoulder too. "Sorry."

Maytag was back in a hurry with the food; handed it to me: two big sandwiches, potato salad, slaw, and beans on a paper plate. All cold. All unbelievably edible. I think I had the first sandwich done before either brother sat down.

Peachy was laughing. "That bovine tranquilizer makes you hungry, too, don' it?"

I nodded, but I was too busy with the slaw to completely answer.

He settled in. His brother was beside him. There was a very pleasant sound of rain on the roof. Otherwise they watched me eat in silence.

Finally Maytag spoke. "So you met Aunt Ida. Daddy said she tried to tell you everything."

I talked around a forkful of beans. "That's quite a system she's got."

Peachy smiled. "You mean the tappin' an' whatnot?"

I nodded.

Maytag shifted into a slouch. "She makes herself known."

I nodded again. "It was interesting. She born mute?"

Peachy looked over at his brother. "Tell 'im."

Maytag closed his eyes. "Naw. You."

Peachy settled in. "Okay. You done eatin'?"

I looked down. The plate was entirely clean, like nothing had ever been there. "Unless I eat the plate—which I might. Why?"

"I get you somethin' else, or you can listen to the story."

I set the plate aside. "Maybe I can get something more in a minute. I'm always willing to take a story break."

Peachy agreed. "Okay."

He set the stage with silence and the drumming of the rain. It was the perfect curtain raiser. Then he let loose with his story.

20

A Kiss in the Cemetery

In their younger days Aunt Ida and her sister were growing up in Savannah. Their father was away in the Navy fighting World War II. He'd promised to return, but the rumor was that his ship had been lost at sea.

Every day the girls walked home from school by a cemetery. The cemetery had gravestones from the Revolutionary War. It was very old.

One day in October Ida's sister was kept after for whispering in class, and had to clean erasers. She'd been whispering to a little cloth-and-wood doll that she kept in her pocket—something her father had given her before he'd gone—and the teacher had caught her and punished her.

Ida waited on the school steps. The day got dark and evening was drawing on. Still, the girls had to play their special game. Every day on their way home from school, they played a game of Dare. People said it was because their father was gone that they were growing up contrary. Nevertheless, challenges were issued in their game. One girl had to run through the Old Baptist Cemetery and touch the back door of the church without making a sound. No screaming allowed. That was the strictest rule: no noise. They didn't want to be caught and get in trouble.

Ida's sister was in a bad mood from her punishment, and she issued a particularly mean challenge that day: Skip through the graveyard, kiss the back door of the church, do a dance on the steps, and then run back—here was the hardest part—jumping over any open graves on the way out. Finally: kiss the little wooden doll. Then they could go home.

Ida was equal to the task, loathe as she was to being called a sissy little girl. She set her books down in the twilight and skipped into the old churchyard. She was very proud of the way she seemed so unafraid, but the cool air and the shadows made the place stranger than ever before.

Arriving at the back door of the church, Ida kissed it, looked to her sister and waved, then danced the new dance they'd seen on television, called the Twist. It made her laugh, and her sister, way off at the street, was laughing too.

Ida spotted an open grave, and determined to leap over it on her triumphal egress. She took a deep breath and headed straight for it, running as fast as she could.

But just as she came to the edge of it, something gray and huge raised up out of the open grave and made a horrible sound. Ida leaped up over it; she was too close to do anything else. But she stumbled on the other side, tripped over a magnolia root, and came down on the ground hard, smashing her head on a carved stone angel at the foot of the next grave site. She lay unconscious. Her sister stood screaming from the street.

Up out of the hole, the poor old man who took care of the place threw himself. He had just finished digging the new grave after a day of planting pansies all around the church.

He was crying. He thought the little girl was dead. He just stood over her saying, "I'm sorry. I'm sorry."

Finally someone came out of the church, and Ida's sister rushed in. They all stood around Ida, afraid to even touch her. The old man said he'd been working when he heard a noise that frightened him. Something flew over his head, and he thought it might be a giant bat. The little girl never made a sound.

Ida's sister stood whispering frantically to the little doll.

Then, in the next moment, Ida opened her eyes. She sat up and smiled. Everyone thanked God. The old man picked her up in his arms and carried her home, with her sister leading the way.

And despite everything medical science could do, Ida kept right on playing the game for the rest of her days: running through the graveyard of her life without making a sound.

From that day on she never spoke another word.

21

Promises

Just in case I was confused, Maytag thought he ought to clarify. "See, that's our Aunt Ida and our Momma. The sister was Momma. Momma used to tell everybody after that happened that she and Ida was one person—half that could talk and half that couldn't."

I nodded. "Right."

Peachy sat back. "Momma always felt guilty, they say. Said it was her doin' that made 'em so late, the whole thing was her fault. She felt sad and sorry and tried to give Ida all kinds of help, you know. They were near inseparable after that night. They did everything together." He gave his brother a very meaningful look, I thought. "Everything."

Maytag continued. "It was what Daddy called a *traumatic event*. See, in the full daylight it ain't so bad, but it's real spooky in the evenin'. We been there. We seen the angel."

Peachy smiled. "Angel that took Ida's voice."

I sat back. "Right. And she started tapping and clicking after that?"

Maytag answered. "Not right away. Took awhile."

Peachy had a theory. "I believe it was seein' that old movie about Macaroni that did it."

I didn't understand right away. "Macaroni?"

He nodded. "That invented the telegraph."

I smiled. "Oh, yeah. *Marconi*."

He was amiable. "Whatever."

"Your aunt saw some movie about Marconi and decided to . . . it's not Morse code she uses?"

"Naw, it's all Ida."

I should have known better, but I had to ask again. "How did you all learn it?"

Maytag volunteered. "We read her mind, most times. We just let 'er tap so she'll feel like she's expressin' herself."

I nodded, trying hard not to think about it too much. "Right. You all read her mind."

Peachy yawned. "We're a close family."

"Uh-huh."

Maytag swatted at his brother. "Mr. Tucker ain't got no normal family. It ain't polite to lord it over 'im."

Peachy closed his eyes. "Oh. Sorry." Then he opened them. "Sorry, Mr. Tucker."

I shrugged. "It's okay. What makes you think I've got no normal family?"

Maytag thought that was pretty good. "Shoot. If you had a family like ours, you'd have a lots a better things to do than run around lookin' for *us*. You got the look of a fella that's unattached."

I settled back again. "Well—I read a lot about how nonattachment is supposed to be enlightening."

Peachy looked at his brother, on the verge of a small satori himself. "Maybe it's like how it is with us an' Momma." He looked at me. "Lots a people thinks we oughta be sad about her dyin'? But we ain't that much attached to her memory an' all."

Maytag looked at me. "We never spent a minute worryin' about—or wishin' Momma had of lived. She didn't. That's all there is to that. Anyway, Ida's been pretty clear with us—ever since we was little-bitty— about what happens to you after you die."

I crossed my arms. "Okay, I'll bite. What happens to you after you die?"

He opened up his hand and showed me his palm. Then he smiled. It was the famous peace that passeth understanding. You get it in nearly all of your better religions.

I nodded. "I see." But maybe I didn't.

The rain was drawing to a conclusion, and it changed the mood in the room. There was even a little low golden light coming in the kitchen window.

Peachy sighed. "I love this time a day."

Maytag leaned over to me. "So, Mr. Tucker—you gonna help us find Lydia or not?"

"Did she kill her husband?"

Peachy drew in a big breath through his nose. "We don't really know. She whispered somethin' in his ear, and after he had time to think about it, he just fell over."

Maytag agreed. "Just like in the storybook we got her for Christmas."

Peachy smiled. "It was a book with English and

Irish stories in it. Lots of folks hereabouts got all kinds of Irish and English in us. That one story's about this spirit of the ocean? And she falls in love with a rich man on the land."

Maytag shook his head. "But it don't work out between 'em."

Peachy nodded. "She just whispered a word in his ear, and he fell right over."

I couldn't tell if they were talking about the story they'd read, or what had happened in the bank in Tifton.

Maytag shifted comfortably. "They tell us he was dead after that. Reckon he got to thinkin' about how bad he'd been—*that's* probably what killed 'im." He stared at nothing for a beat or two. "So how you gonna find 'er, Mr. Turner?"

Peachy was interested too. "What exactly does a person in your line of work actually *do*?"

I looked out at the golden kitchen. "Often I use the same method that I so successfully employed to find the two of *you*."

Peachy blinked. "What was that?"

"I let *you* come to *me*."

Maytag agreed. "That's a way to do it."

Peachy nodded his head slowly. "Take 'er easy." But he seemed distracted for a second.

Maytag looked around strangely, too, and then he hoisted himself up. "I'm goin' to bed."

I checked my watch. "It's not even seven."

He didn't look back at me. "We didn't sleep last night."

Peachy looked over at his brother and nodded.

"You got a nice long sleep, but we didn't sleep at all."

I tightened my lips. "Yeah. I had it lucky." Something was up with them, but I couldn't tell what it was.

Maytag was headed up the stairs. "You could try to call your lady friend again."

Peachy followed. "Make you a bed there on the sofa."

Maytag disappeared around the top of the steps. "See you later."

Peachy looked back. "Or, I reckon you could watch the TV an' all. It gets all kinds of channels." He paused a moment on the top step. "So you gonna help us? We really gotta find her in the worstest way."

"I'll do what I can." There. I'd said it. Now I actually had to do something about it.

I guess it was good enough for him; he understood the nature of the promise. He was gone too. The idea I'd had in the back of my head about being kidnapped for some sinister reason by lunatic farmer boys was evaporating pretty quickly. I really could have split then if I'd wanted to—plenty of evening light left in the long summer day. But I'd made my promise, so I stuck to it. I never *think* making a promise like that will get me into trouble, but it usually does.

22

Boom

I reached for the phone; dialed.

The answer: "DeSoto Beach Motel."

"Twenty-seven."

Pause.

"Hello?"

"Dally, it's me again."

She was anxious. "Flap. What happened? You okay?"

"Started storming, that's all. We got cut off. I'm great."

"Except for the fact that you got some kinda god-awful drug in you and you're kidnapped by retarded farm boys."

"They're not retarded, they're simple. They were very clear on that issue."

"Are they listening?"

I settled back in my chair. "They're asleep."

"So . . . if you wanted to, could you leave now?"

"Yup."

"But you're stayin'?"

"Uh-huh."

She sounded more relieved. "So you really are okay."

"I really am okay."

She let out a big breath. "Good."

"So what's all this frantic talk about something strange with our current investigation? You were talking maybe a little crazy before."

"What?"

"Before you hung up, you were wild to tell me something about all this business that you hadn't told me before."

"Oh. Yeah. Prob'ly just the drugs."

"So, you're not going to tell me now?"

"You're really okay? I mean—they're not holding a gat on you or anything?"

"Gat?"

"You heard me."

"No. No gats, no roscoes, no equalizers, no persuaders, no blue steel babies."

"Plus," she shifted the phone, "no guns, right?"

I had to laugh. "Yeah, no guns. So come on, tell me the deal."

"I don't want to now."

I couldn't believe it. "What?"

"If you really are okay, I'd rather wait until I see you in person. Which'll be *when*, by the way?"

"I dunno. I gotta help the boys find Lydia now."

"Why?"

"That's what they want me to do, and I'm inclined to do it."

"Oh." But she wanted to say more, I could tell.

"So you're not going to tell me what's up?"

Silence.

"Dally?"

More silence. Then: "Flap, you gotta talk to me before you go lookin' for Lydia, okay?"

I shifted the phone. "What for?"

She was stubborn. "Sorry."

"Be sorry all you want; tell me what's going on."

"In the words of the immortal Marvin Gaye."

"Stop it."

"You'll be mad."

"I won't be mad."

"Yes you will."

I shifted the phone again; leaned forward. "Dally, this is absolutely and uncharacteristically . . . excuse my language: *feminine* of you. It's making me nervous. I've got enough yang in my diet."

"I see no reason to insult me with this *yang* talk. And by the way, God forbid I should seem *feminine* to you."

"Who is this?"

"What?"

"Who am I talking to?" I leaned farther forward.

Pause. She spoke softer. "I know. I'm sorry. The hangover from these pills is makin' me a little wacky. How many'd they give me, you know?"

"They said five."

"What was it?"

"They didn't say that part. Some prescription from their father."

She got even softer. "I'm worried about you and I'm . . . talkin' all wrong."

I relaxed a little too. "*You're* talking wrong? I got a cow in my head."

"So."

"So, you're really not going to tell me any more right now . . . so, okay."

She spoke very softly. "Just . . . this all might have something to do with *your* past."

"*My* past?"

"Maybe it does, and maybe it doesn't. That's all I'm gonna say till I see you face-to-face—you big lug."

I smiled. When Dalliance doesn't want to talk, she doesn't. "Big lug?"

"In keeping with the *gat* and *roscoe* motif."

"Ah."

And *boom* there was a noise in the kitchen the size of the Fourth of July. I nearly dropped the phone.

Dally heard it over the receiver. "What the *hell* was that?"

"Shhh." I put the phone down.

Glass breaking, big pops, snarling voices, running—something big bashing at the door: it had all the jolly earmarks of a bust.

I quick turned on more lights so that they could see me really well, and put both my hands up on my head; stood very still. In an ear-busting crack the door was kindling, and five or six guys imitating the cops they'd seen on television came savaging in, growling and hustling to beat the band.

Flashlights were all over me, even though they didn't need them. Big fat *angry* guys were yelling at me to stand still, get down, put my hands on my head, put my hands behind my back, answer questions, shut up—all manner of oxymorons. And I use the term advisedly.

"Lie flat on the floor and stand still!" My favorite.

I didn't want to be a smart guy, but around these goons I didn't have a choice. "Which is it, lie down or stand still?"

"Shut up!"

I did. Several were still pointing their guns at me. Most were running up the stairs, yelling. In my experience you only yelled like that when you were scared. I didn't mean to be hard on the guys. Being a cop was tough, and if you had any sense, you'd *better* be scared most of the time. But these guys were playing cops. As I was saying, I blamed television.

"Nobody else in the house!"

That got me. Where had those Turner boys gotten off to?

Somebody came in the remains of the front door. He was moving slow, so I was guessing he was older, or in charge—or just didn't watch as much TV as the rest of the merry band.

I couldn't see him well because of the light in my face, but the voice was familiar.

"So, Mr. Tucker. Where have those Turner boys gotten off to?"

I squinted. "Hey, Tommy? That's you?"

"Detective Acree."

"Uh-huh."

"Where are the boys?"

"They went up to bed about two minutes ago."

He hollered, "Nobody in the bedrooms?"

Pause. Then: "No, sir! The house is empty."

I couldn't resist. "Except . . . for me."

Tommy wasn't all that impressed with my humor. "We know those boys got you out of The Hut. We know they drugged you and kidnapped you. What we don't know is why."

The light was really getting to me. "Oh, there's a lot more you don't know. You don't know where the boys are now, for instance. And you're mistaken about the kidnapping. I'm here of my own free will. As to the drug thing, I've been having a little trouble sleeping lately, and they gave me a sedative, that's all."

He was still calm, which surprised me. "We saw them cart you out of the restaurant. They poisoned you. It might've killed you."

"Naw. Just got a good night's sleep."

He pushed. "On a boat."

"You know I think that did help matters, come to think of it. The rocking motion on a boat is very soothing."

"They dragged you out of The Hut like a sack a potatoes. They carried Ms. Oglethorpe to her room and took you on a boat. I'm tryin' to give you a break, Mr. Tucker. I'm willin' to believe you're a victim or a dupe of these criminals. But if you like, I can treat you as an accomplice."

"Accomplice to what?"

He was plain. "The murder of Lowe Acree."

I smiled. "Except for the fact that there's not a shred of what we call *evidence* in the police game. By the way, I'm having the body exhumed." I thought it was a good bluff—see what it would get me. "Your cousin died of an aneurysm."

He finally lost his cool, which had been my goal. "Now you're a doctor?" He swatted at one of the cops standing next to him. "Get those flashlights off him!" He whirled back at me. "Sit down and shut up. You'll be *president* before you get an order to exhume my cousin's body."

The lights went out of my face; I sat back down in my chair. The phone was still off the hook.

I raised my voice. "So, Detective Acree—where are we, exactly? The boys were a little fuzzy on the geography. I was guessing Cumberland."

But he was in no mood to give out information. He looked at the cop he'd just swatted. "If he talks any more, shoot him in the head with a really big gun."

The boy nodded smartly. "Yes, sir."

Tommy was off, lumbering up the stairs. I looked at the cop standing there beside me. I smiled and whispered at him. "He was just kiddin'—about that really-big-gun thing."

The kid didn't see the humor. That's my doom: Nobody thinks I'm as funny as I do. I decided to try to give Dally as much information as I could before somebody hung up the phone.

I looked at the kid. "Swell house, huh."

He didn't answer.

I looked around. "I don't think the Turner twins own it, though."

He rolled his eyes.

My suspicion was that he was just out of high school. He was a small-town assistant deputy who spent most of his day doing what he was told.

I yawned. "I think this house is owned by Lydia Habersham."

"I don't really think I should be talkin' to you."

"Okay."

He yawned.

Tommy saved us from further scintillating conversation. From the top of the stairs he called out to me. "Mr. Tucker? Would you mind joining us up here?"

I looked at the kid. I didn't want to make any sudden moves around him. He might just have had a really big gun handy. Besides, I've taken to making funny noises when I get up out of my chair these days. I'm pretty sure they're the same noises my father used to make. I didn't want to startle the assistant deputy.

He nodded. I got up. He took my arm, like we were going to the prom, and we both started up the staircase. I glanced at the phone, still off the hook. "Okay. Upstairs." I was hoping Dally was getting all this.

Tommy had disappeared into one of the rooms. "In here."

I followed. It was a nice place: antique white, faintly gold, Lincoln bed, hook rug; a marble-topped table supported an ancient wash bowl and pitcher. The bed was messed up but still fresh, crisp. Somebody had laid down, and got right back up, like they wanted to make it look slept in.

Tommy leaned on the foot of the bed. "Which one slept here?"

"I don't know. This is my first visit to the second floor. We only just got here. By the way, have you had a guy following me since I left Tifton?"

He nodded. "Just about. You're some detective. Didn't even notice a cheap amateur tail."

I shrugged. "The tail picked me up in Savannah. Nobody was following me on the drive over those little roads coming here."

He stood straight. "Didn't have to be. Ronnie Tibadeau put a pulse emitter under your chassis. It was real cheap. I bought parts and made it myself. I'm a kind of Saturday inventor."

"Ronnie Tibadeau put a bug in my car?"

"Oh, he's too stupid to know what he was doing. I told him it was something you'd asked for, in case you got lost. He'll do anything I tell him. Used to kind of work for Lowe. Plus, as you may have noticed, he's about a dumb as the law allows."

"They got a law about that in Tifton?"

He ignored me. "So you really don't know whose room this is?"

"Nope. I just met the boys. I just got to the house. I'm still cranky from the cow juice. *And* I'm kicking myself for not paying attention when I get paranoid."

"Oh, so now you're trying to say you *did* notice the tail."

"I'm *trying* to say I wish I were home in bed."

"Yeah, well I wish you were too. You're complicating the situation here."

I looked around the room. "I've got certain talents. I could actually be of some help to you."

He smiled and shook his head. "I've heard about some of those so-called talents, Mr. Tucker. We have no need of hocus-pocus on this investigation."

I thought about it for a second. "How would you have heard anything about me?"

He looked away. I couldn't tell if it was because he didn't want me to see his face or he didn't care. "Sally Arnold."

She wouldn't know, but I didn't want to get into a thing with the guy. He might get the idea I'm the sort that likes to get into things, and then where would I be?

He turned around to face me. "I'm going to send you back to your hotel room now, and I wish you'd pack and return to Atlanta with Ms. Oglethorpe."

I shrugged. "Dally's got business here. She's starting a club on River Street. She'll be staying for a while."

"Is that right?"

"She's not just a fine person, she's an entrepreneur."

He looked right past me to the kid who'd escorted me up the stairs. "Take him back to the DeSoto. Wait for us in town. You know where." He said it like a spy thing.

The kid hesitated. "Uh . . . in-town-Tybee or in-town-Savannah?"

Tommy sighed, his spy lingo blown. "At the place in Savannah."

The kid was anxious to leave then. "Right, right." He grabbed my arm and started out, but I stood my ground and he slipped a little on the hook rug.

I fixed on Tommy. "I still have work to do here, Detective Acree."

He was wry. "You found the boys. Call it a day."

I shook my head. "I've still got to find Lydia."

He got stranger. "No, you don't."

"I promised."

"I don't care if you *promised*. Who'd you promise? The twins?"

"Look, if I said I was going do it, I've got to do it. It's a *thing* with me. It's like a sickness."

He looked at the kid again—seriously mad at that point. "Take him back to his room. Watch him pack. Escort him to his car—that's very important—escort him to his car. See that he *leaves town*. Then you can meet us at the place we discussed." He shot me a glance. "Good-bye, Mr. Tucker. I got to catch me some murdering retards, and you have ceased to be amusing."

I saw how things were. I nodded. The kid looked at me now, begging me to just come along with him and not make him look any stupider than he already looked—which would have been going some. I shrugged. It's a good expression. The French do it a lot. When I caught myself doing it, I started thinking maybe there was something to this heritage thing after all.

On the way out I checked again—but somebody had hung up the phone by then.

23

The Golden Code

The ride back to Tybee in the police boat was swell.
It was just me, the driver, and the kid. Nobody
wanted to talk, so I had time to reflect. The sun was
getting fresh with the western horizon—the sky was
blushing red and pink. I was worried about all manner of things, but the sunset was working on me. I
was thinking how a long, slow, summer sunset was
just the ticket. I was watching the water. I was thinking about my childhood—something I never do.
Why was the idea of *that* scratching at the back of
my neck?

We docked just as the last of the light was gone. I
never got from anybody what island we'd been on.
The kid looked at me like I was a wicked messenger—
the personification of bad news.

"You ain't gonna need the cuffs, Mr. Tucker,
huh?"

I smiled. "What am I going to need cuffs for?"

He was relieved. We got to a police car; he slammed me into the front seat, a friendly touch. We drove without talking any more, straight to the motel. I waited for him to get out and open my door, like we were dating in high school.

Up the stairs I stopped at the door.

He sighed. "You ain't got the key?"

I smiled again. "Just don't want to surprise Ms. Oglethorpe. She may be indisposed."

He nodded, quick. "Right, right."

I tapped on the door. No answer. I tried again. Nothing. I reached into my pocket and hauled out the key. I popped the lock, cracked the door, peeped in.

"Dally?"

Still no answer. One of the lamps was on, and underneath it was a notepad with some writing on it. I stepped in and headed for it before the kid could get a look.

It was a note from Dally:

> Gone Over Loading Dock. Everything's Negotiable.
> Come. Urgent: Remember Tell Aunt Ida Now.
>
> D.O.
>
> P.S. After all that, we need to talk about the other stuff,
> Or maybe by then you'll know.

I had to laugh out loud. The kid snatched the note and read it himself. He didn't see the humor.

"What's funny?"

I took the note back from him. "I'm just glad she's okay; back to work and all."

But the truth was: Using a code as ridiculous as
the first letter in every word of the message, and cap-
italized at that, to tell me what she thought I ought
to do—that was pretty funny indeed. Even the kid
could have figured it o<u>ut</u>. But if he had, *Golden Curtain* wouldn't have meant anything to him anyway.
The whole deal was her corny little joke. Dally loved
the spy talk. Not the James Bond, more the John le
Carré. Spy talk is largely for people who'd like to
think their lives are more interesting than they actually are. In Dally's case, however, it was always a
comedy routine: talking in pig Latin like it was a secret language; leaving notes like this one. Once she
just about slayed me faking a distraction so that she
could slip an extra pack of sugar in my coffee, like it
was a mickey. I couldn't stop laughing. It was when
we were in high school, before the world got old. But
I reminisce.

So why did she do it? Why did she leave me a
note like that one? She could have just said, "Do the
Golden Curtain thing, then we'll talk." Nobody but I
would have known what she was talking about anyway. She wanted me to think about the sugar-pack
mickey. She wanted me to think about goofy covert
activity, like Detective Acree and his secret ren-
dezvous place that the kid had messed up. She
wanted me to think about the past—my past.

Why? I had no idea. And why did she sign it
with her initials? Why sign it at all? She was the only
one in the room who'd be leaving me a note, and
I knew her handwriting as well as my own. I considered it just might have been her penchant for
a good story, but for some reason I got the idea

it was a little more urgent than that. I mean, it said, "DO."

I looked at the kid. "Look, you're a youngster, and you've got energy to burn, but me, I'm getting past my prime and I need a minute to rest up from my hectic day. I've been drugged, kidnapped, busted, lied to, and hustled outta town. I need a little time to lie down, change clothes; freshen up before I drive back to Atlanta. Okay? You can wait right out here in this nice little room. I won't be more than half an hour, forty-five minutes. Then I'll pack and be outta your hair. If you hear the slightest noise that bothers you, come busting in on me with your really big gun quick as you please. What do you say?"

He hesitated, peered into the bedroom to make sure there wasn't an exit door, looked at the window to see was it locked, looked out at the ocean from the nice big bay window where he was standing.

"An' after that you'll leave nice?"

I nodded. "I've just got to have a break."

He thought about it one more minute. "Okay, then."

He crossed his arms, kept standing, and watched me walk into the bedroom and close the door. He was a good kid after all.

I couldn't figure why Dally thought it was so important for me to do my thing right that second. But she did, and I was bound to go along with it. She knew what she was doing—nearly all the time.

I took a moment or two so as to splash a little water around and change the old outfit. Then I sat on the edge of the bed looking out at the sea. This little trick of mine, it's not so particular, really. I'd like to think nearly anybody could do it if they'd give it half the chance. It's probably nothing more than a way to relax enough to let your mind tell you the stuff it's been trying to tell you all day but you've been too busy to listen. So you have to be quiet and relax.

You stare out. If you're lucky enough to be at the beach, you stare out at the ocean. You breathe in, you breathe out. You see how your breathing is like the sound of the waves. You see how your breath and the waves and the whole wide world are all pretty much the same thing. After a while, there's nothing but the breathing. That's the touchy part. You can't make it happen. You just have to let it happen. If it does, you can't congratulate yourself: "Look, I got a vision!" That's the last thing you want to do. It goes away if you do that. It goes away if you mess with it at all. But if you're quiet, and if you're still, it comes to you easy, like breathing out and breathing in.

And there it was, a kind of gold fog. Dimly at first, I could see people walking back and forth through it. Lots of people. They were all greeting one another in a very friendly fashion. They were all families. It was a family reunion. Old friends, old acquaintances, distant relatives, new babies—everybody was there, sitting around tables, eating fried chicken.

At one table were the Turner twins and their family, Ida tapping out a complicated rhythm with her knife and fork. Next to them was Pevus Arnold and a woman I took to be his wife, a little like a plump Joseph and Mary; Sally Arnold hovering over them with more fried chicken.

At the far end of the yard Dally was waving me over. She was at a table with Lydia. I still couldn't see her face, but I could tell it was her from the wispy blond hair drifting all around her like the light of grace.

From a distance she waved, and said, "Hello, Flap. Good to see you again."

Then, sneaking around the corner of the church, I saw two young girls—I had the impression they were sisters. They were playing with a doll—a magic doll that could talk. They held it up, and one girl said, "Say hello to Lydia."

Then, from behind me I heard another voice. I turned around. It was Horace the curbside drug tradesman from Atlanta. I nodded. He seemed to want something from me.

He was motioning me over to the graveyard by the church. It was dark and filled with open graves and magnolia trees. Lowe Acree was popping up out of one of the graves, like a strange repeated act at a carnival haunted house. Lydia was standing by a stone angel, laughing and laughing and laughing.

After a minute she and Horace went to Lowe's graveside. Lowe smiled and slid back down in the grave. Horace wandered off in a northerly direction. Lydia ran over to the Turner table, laid on it face-down, and pretended to be swimming.

I came over to stop her, since no one else seemed able to do it. When I got there, still with her face turned away, she said, "Hello, Flap. Good to see you again."

The voice sounded so familiar, it set me spinning.

24

Songs of Shakespeare

I was startled from my reverie. The kid in the other room had gotten impatient. Apparently he'd knocked quietly on the door, but when I'm in the middle of my trick, I can't hear much unless it's really loud.

He'd slipped open the door, caught sight of the back of my head, tiptoed in to tell me it was time to go, and seen me staring blankly out to sea.

He was shaking me like a rag doll. "Mr. Tucker! Mr. Tucker!"

I blinked; sighed. He stopped shaking me. I squinted at him. "A simple 'wake up' would suffice."

He was pretty well flustered. "You was asleep? You sleep with your eyes open?"

I rubbed my face. "Sorta."

"Well . . . Lordy, mister." I could still see the panic on his face.

I had no sympathy. "You woke me up out of a kind of important dream."

"I thought you was dead." He leaned back against the windowsill.

"I wasn't." I bobbed up out of the chair. "So. Guess I better pack."

I got all my stuff together in a hurry. He watched, still a little shaky. I finished, straightened my tie, hoisted my coat over my shoulder like Sinatra, and smiled at him.

"Guess we'll leave Ms. Oglethorpe's stuff to her."

He nodded.

I started out. "I gotta stop by the bar. Gotta pick up my potables."

"Huh?"

"My comestibles."

"Mr. Tucker . . ."

"I've got some bottles in the bar downstairs that I'm not leaving behind." I opened the door to the room. "Coming?"

He sighed like it was the end of the world, and we headed downstairs. June wasn't busy.

She eyed me, then the kid, then me again. "Hey, Taylor."

The kid looked down. "Hey, Ms. June."

She looked at me. "What can I do for you, Mr. Tucker?"

"You could lay off telling my fortune, quit recommending places for dinner, and give me what's left of my Château Simard."

She looked down. "I did it for Lydia, you know."

I softened. "I know. My wine."

She nodded. "Got about a bottle and a half left here. Twins give you what was left from last night over at The Hut?"

"Yeah. And I'd like not to cart around an open bottle of spirits. It's against the law, they tell me, and Taylor here is an officer in law enforcement. So maybe you could pop the cork on the half bottle and help me finish it up. Kind of a farewell-no-hard-feelings sorta thing."

She liked that. "Dally was right. You're a character."

I heaved myself onto the closest barstool. "That's me. In fact I'm a character in the play in God's mind. Did you know that, June? Just like you. Just like all of us. We can't help it."

She bent over to get the bottles, paying me absolutely no mind.

I looked at Taylor. "So, can you join us, officer?"

He looked around. "I better not."

I turned back to June. "It's not really *drinking* with this stuff, Taylor. It's more like a conversation."

He didn't understand. I didn't feel like explaining anything to either one of them. I was still a little preoccupied by what I'd seen in my little waking dream. It was rare to get a dream like that. Usually it was just a wadded jumble of images. This was like some dream sequence from a Hitchcock film.

June plopped down a full glass in front of me, slid the other unopened bottle toward me, and hoisted her own half-filled glass in the direction of the framed newspaper story on the bar wall behind her.

"Here's to your little adventure on the coast, Flap."

I looked at the frame behind her too. "And to Lydia. 'Who is Lydia, what is she, that all our swains commend her?' You know that?"

June eyed me. "You think I don't know, but I do. It's 'Sylvia.' It's Shakespeare. It's a song."

Taylor nodded, almost to himself, embarrassed to know. "Schubert set it to music."

I set down my glass to eye them both.

Taylor spoke right up. "We got us a great little school system down this way, Mr. Tucker. We're not so stupid as a lotsa people think."

June winked at him. "Taylor here plays the viola, don't you, hon?"

He looked at his feet, like the answer to her question might be written there. "Yes, ma'am."

I got it. "So you played the Schubert in school band or some such."

"Community orchestra, yes, sir. Uh-huh. It was our *Songs of Shakespeare* show."

June nodded. "Well attended."

He still didn't look up. "For a winter show, yes, ma'am."

I looked at him. "Taylor? You know the churchyards over in Savannah? You know one that would have a stone angel and a lot of magnolia trees?"

He finally looked at me. "Don't know one that *wouldn't* be like that."

"Oh."

June sipped. "Prettiest one to me is the one close over there at River Street." She looked to Taylor for guidance. "That's the Old Baptist?"

He nodded. "It's always been kep' up right nice, all those inpatients in the summer and pansies ever'where in the fall."

There it was, the Old Baptist with the pansies out front. There's no such thing as coincidence.

I knocked back a healthy taste of the Simard. "I'll have to catch it sometime."

June set down her glass. "Look, Flap . . . I'm sorry we had to treat you so bad what with sluggin' you out with my own daughter's food and all. I hope you understand. It's Lydia. I care for her more than you can possibly imagine."

I finished off my wine, swiped up the un-opened bottle. "I don't know—I've got a pretty good imagination."

Taylor shifted his weight. "Ready to go, Mr. Tucker?"

"Yup."

We started out, but I couldn't resist the exit music. I popped a quarter in, and mashed good old R2: "Stardust"—for my money, the music of the spheres. It shuffled us out of the lounge with a good bit of class.

25

Carpenters and Masons

Out in the parking lot, I tossed my stuff in the back-seat of my heap, on the rider's side, and waved at Taylor where he was standing by his cop car. He did not wave back. He was a musician, not a police-man, and the disparity between what he loved and what he did for a living made him impolite. It's a common malady. Most men lead lives of quiet impoliteness.

He shot me a look. "I'm following you to the highway. I'm watching you get on. You're going to Atlanta tonight. You'll be home by midnight. I'll call to make sure."

"That's very thoughtful. I am prone to car trouble."

"Good-bye, Mr. Tucker." I could tell he was try-ing to sound like Tommy Acree.

The magic of Ronnie Tibadeau was in evidence still. I got cranked the first turn, and my car was rolling. True to his promise, Taylor followed close behind. He was with me up the ramp to the interstate. He followed past the first exit, the second exit. Just when I thought he might tail me halfway to Atlanta, he flashed his lights and roared past me, slipped into a police turnaround in the median, and zoomed away back toward Savannah.

I rolled on to the next stop, got off, pulled into a station; slipped under the car. There it was, plain as day: some cheap, homemade gizmo. I didn't know whether it was still working or not, but I popped it off anyway. Just for laughs, I slipped it under the bumper of a station wagon with Michigan plates while the owner was paying for his gas.

Then I got in my car and headed back into Savannah to look for an Old Baptist graveyard. June had said the church in question was near River Street. At least I knew where *that* was; that's where I headed. Found a parking place up on the street that overlooked the docks. Just for old times' sake I wandered down onto River Street itself, looking for the ghosts of days gone by.

Sure enough, there was the place where the Night Flight used to be. And inside, there was activity, lights, something happening. I peered in the window. True to her wacky note, there was Dally, ordering some schmo around.

I tapped on the glass, they both looked. Dally came to the door a little quicker than she usually moves, and popped it open.

"Took you long enough to get here."

"I got run outta town by Johnny Law."

"But it didn't take, did it?"

I smiled. "Here I am."

"Well, I guess you better come in and survey the landscape of your past."

"It has been a while. We had a great gig here once upon a time."

She introduced me to the schmo. "This is Homer. He's a cabinetmaker. He apprenticed for twelve years. He's good."

He nodded.

I let him get back to his wandering, and motioned Dally over to a spot where the bar used to be. "Nice note you left me."

She grinned. "Yeah. I thought you'd find it amusing."

"What's the deal?"

She took a deep breath. "Know how you're always mouthin' off about life bein' like a game?"

"Thanks for paying attention. Like a *play*."

"Whatever. I kind of got a dose of it at the moment."

"Sorry. I didn't figure it to be contagious."

"Yeah, well—I'm giddy."

I had no idea what she was getting at. "Okay."

"It all seems a little like a game to me."

"And by *all* you mean . . . ?"

She wouldn't answer me. "You do your thing yet?"

"Yeah. But I didn't finish. I got interrupted before anything made any sense."

"What was it?"

"Family reunion."

She was cagey. "Really."

"Is that supposed to mean something?"

"You bet."

"Such as?"

She looked around the room. "You guys played here, huh?"

I nodded. "Yeah. It was a dream gig. A week at the beach, seafood every day, fishing for blue crabs off the peer. And I had a little thing for the assistant manager."

"Is that right?"

"I don't know whether it was *right* or not, but it was swell. She was engaged to the manager, I think, but he was outta town. She was sowing her wild oats. Or would it be sea oats out here?"

"She took advantage of you."

"Oh, yeah."

She smiled. "And it lasted . . . ?"

I nodded. "An entire week. Right after we left town, there was a kind of bad hurricane. Did a lot of damage out on Tybee."

"You never know what kinda damage you leave behind you when you're young, do you?"

I looked at her. She was somewhere else, staring off into space. I hated to bother her—wherever she was—but it was uncharacteristic. "You reminisce."

She came back. "Yeah. I do."

I reached out and got ahold of her elbow. "Well, knock it off. The past, as they say, is only prologue . . . you know."

"Yeah. I know."

"So."

She rallied. "So."

"I gotta find a church graveyard."

She blinked. "Because?"

"Because I have the intuition I'll find the mysterious Lydia there."

"Well, that's a kind of far-fetched notion, don't you think?"

I agreed. "But my notions can fetch pretty far, don't you think?"

She thought for a second. "Okay. Where is it?"

"Around here somewhere. It's tied in with the Turners' Aunt Ida. It's where she lost her voice."

I told her the story. She enjoyed it. I've mentioned how she'll always go for a story.

Homer overheard. "Y'all are talkin' about the *Old* Old Baptist."

I turned to him. "As opposed to . . ."

He smiled. "Just the plain Old Baptist, which, see, it just got built after the Civil War. The *Old* Old Baptist was built before the Revolution."

I looked at Dally. "They got buildings around here that old?"

He was certain. "Yes, sir. That ain't nothin'. See, in America, you get to be old after a hundred years or so. But over there in Europe? Shoot. You gotta be five hundred 'fore they even take you serious. They got a lotsa *old* over there."

I was impressed. "Nice work, Homer. I heard they had a great school system around here."

He was proud. "Ah, most of what I know is from the guy I's apprenticed to. He's from England? He learned it from his great uncle, who learned it from somebody else in the family, and on and on back to Noah."

"Noah?"

He explained it to me. "Yes, sir. Noah? He was a carpenter back in the Bible."

"Yeah, I know who Noah is."

Homer tried to take it all in. "I didn't ever think he was from England, though."

I looked at Dally. "Me either."

Dally encouraged Homer to more talk. "Tell him why you got to apprentice with him, Homer."

"Oh. Well, he ain't got no kids, and no kin that's interested in the work. He's a Mason?"

I didn't get it. "Like a Shriner?"

"Naw. That's his name. He's related to the actor James Mason."

Dally was the only vocal skeptic. "So he tells Homer, anyway."

Homer was undaunted by Dally's cynicism. "Don't matter if it's true. It makes a good story. And he's a great carpenter. Best I ever saw. He knows stuff about buildin' that a lots of people's forgot." Homer squinted. "An' now he's got nobody to pass it on to but me. Ain't none of the rest of his family the least little bit interested in all that know-how." He looked at me. "Don't people over there in England care about the family?"

Like I'd know.

Dally was more practical. "So, which way to the cemetery?"

He motioned us over. "Look." He started drawing us a little map on a yellow pad. "It's just right up there."

He pointed in the direction of the sea.

26

Poets and Thieves

It was plenty dark by the time Dally had finished describing the perfect nightclub to Homer. They discussed it, then he left; we locked up and headed toward the graveyard, walking.

The streetlights kept the moon from seeming too bright. It was nearly full. Full moon on the way to the boneyard. You had to admit that the author of the play had a sense of humor.

We arrived. It was well kept and lousy with historical markers in front. Nobody was home. We ambled on around the back. It was darker outside the range of the streetlights and underneath the old live oaks and Spanish moss. Magnolias were nearly solid all around the older part of the digs. The smell of the blossoms was everywhere.

It got to me. "Man. Is magnolia the greatest smell or what?"

She was quiet. "Shhh. How in the world are you

gonna find this Lydia if you clump around smellin'
the flowers and yakkin'?"

"A lot of people would say that's the best way to
find a woman."

"Hush."

We walked around for a good while; found some
Revolutionary War heroes, according to the markers.
Even after dark the place was steamy hot. After a
while we sat down on one of the benches for a
breather.

I felt like musing. The full moon and the environs
made it seem appropriate. "I ever tell you what happened at Verlaine's funeral?"

She shook her head.

I settled in. "There was a tug-of-war between his
publisher and his mistress over who was going to get
his winding-sheet. During the ruckus a man named
Louis Ai stole fourteen umbrellas. That's what the
French newspapers said when they were writing Verlaine's obituary."

"Umbrellas?"

"The mourners at the funeral had left a bunch of
them leaning against a tree."

She nodded. "Know what *umbrella* means? It's
from the Latin *umbra,* meaning 'shadow'; the di-
minutive is *umbelia,* meaning 'the little shadow.' So I
guess you're not the only font of knowledge in *this*
couple."

I smiled. "I guess not."

Then, quietly: "Why bring up Verlaine?"

I shrugged. "A—a great French poet. B—pals
with Rimbaud—"

She interrupted. ". . . until Verlaine gets him in some fight and Verlaine goes to jail over it."

I ignored. "C—converted to Catholicism in jail, so you know he's *serious*. D—ideal Symbolist poet."

"So you bring him up because . . ."

I nodded. ". . . he's a major figure in nineteenth-century literature."

She took it all in. "I see. Know what happened at my grandmother's funeral?"

"Okay, what?"

"They had a drawing and gave away a door prize."

"Really."

"Trip to Bermuda."

"I hear it's a paradise on earth."

She eyed me. "It is. That was the symbolism. We're lousy with symbolists in our family, too, so shove the fancy talk. Honestly. You got way too much free time."

"Okay."

We sat in silence for a minute or two. The fireflies were like sparklers. Finally she shifted in her seat. "How do you spell his name?"

"V-e-r—"

"No, not the poet, the umbrella thief."

"A-i."

"That's it? A-i?"

"Yup."

"The way you pronounced it, I thought it was . . . what's the French word for 'garlic'?"

"A-i-l."

"Yeah. I thought the guy's last name was 'garlic.'"

A name like that could turn anybody to a life of crime. Louey Garlic."

I was willing to play. "Yeah, what you name a kid is liable to cause trouble, but you'd think it'd be some kind of culinary crime."

She nodded. "Never can tell what makes a man steal fourteen umbrellas."

I was settling in. "Funny, you know? Some guys are remembered because they wrote great, beautiful words that'll mean something to somebody for a long time—and some are remembered because they stood next to some poet's funeral and stole umbrellas."

And without any kind of warning, there was a voice right behind us.

"Hey, Mr. Tucker."

I was around so fast it knocked the bench over, and Dally went grass surfing.

With his hand out, he tried to calm me. "Whoa back there, hoss."

In the dim light from the nearby streetlamps I could barely make out Maytag Turner. Out of the shadows there was another shape. I could only guess it was Peachy.

I straightened up. "Hey, boys."

Dally sat up. "You all must be the Turner twins."

Maytag was over helping her up with a speed and agility I would not have expected.

I looked at Peachy. "He moves fast for a big boy."

Peachy was proud. "Football."

Maytag was modest. "Peachy's the hero. He was always in the end zone for me."

Peachy wouldn't hear of it. "Maytag come bustin' through any line, stand around long as he wanted.

Nobody could bring 'im down. Then when he felt like it, he'd toss me the ball."

Maytag nodded. "We were a fine team."

Peachy straightened out the bench. "Sorry to sneak up on you all. Didn't mean to scare nobody. We didn't know for sure it'd be y'all."

Maytag explained. "Coulda been somebody on a date."

Peachy was embarrassed. "We didn't wanna disturb nobody."

Maytag had Dally up. "So we had to sneak. Sorry."

I looked at Dally. "This is Ms. Oglethorpe."

Peachy swatted at my arm. "We know."

Maytag made it clear how dumb I was. "Who else would you be out here with?"

Peachy wanted to clear the air. "Y'all missin' some umbrellas?"

I shook my head. "It was a story."

Maytag nodded. "Oh, yeah. Ms. Oglethorpe likes her a story."

Peachy was ready to move on. "Okee-doke. We can go now."

Maytag came over to me. "I'm glad you remembered us tellin' you about Ida's little adventure. Wanna see the angel?"

"Sure." Why not, you know? Part of the Tao thing is letting it all happen around you.

They took us to a newer part of the yard. It was still dark, but you could see the angel. It almost had a glow, a kind of eerie light.

Maytag leaned over to it. "That moss or lichen

that's on it? It's got a kind of a phosphorescence makes it seem kinda like it's glowin' a little, don't it?"

Peachy was a little anxious. "This place gives me the chill bumps. Could we go to a Waffle House or somethin'?"

Maytag looked at me. "We got some talkin' to do."

I agreed. "Yes, we do."

Dally cleared her throat. "Waffle House?"

Peachy shrugged. "Or someplace good. Don't matter. Denny's?"

Dally rolled her eyes. "That's right, boys. Let's go to a well-lit all-night eatery that's a *known* cop hangout. None of the three of you are supposed to be in town, remember? Plus, *two* out of three are supposed to be in jail for *murder*."

Maytag agreed. "Got a point. Where do we go, then?"

Dally smiled. "Too Easy."

27

The Trouble with Mechanics

We started on our way back to Dally's new night-club. I decided I had to go by my car, to get the stuff out and bring it in with me. The boys went on ahead with the key. Dally didn't like them being seen out in plain sight—not with all of us together, especially—but she was impatient. She didn't know why I had to go to the car.

I had facts on my side. "Over fifty percent of all crimes committed in Savannah involve some bum busting in a guy's driver-side window and removing his goods from a car."

She rolled her eyes. "Like anybody's gonna want your crummy stuff."

We sidled up to the vehicle in question. Dally stood on the rider's side, arms folded, tapping her foot like Krupa.

I shoved myself around to the driver's side. There they were. The unmistakable legs of that magic mechanic, Ronnie Tibadeau. He was in evidence, but very still, like I'd seen him before.

"What's up under there now, Ron—more surveillance equipment?"

Dally was confused. "Huh?"

Ronnie, he didn't say a word. In fact he was a whole bunch of stillness. I nudged his leg with my foot. It flopped.

Now she was irritated. "What're you doin', Flap?"

I looked up at her. "Uh, hon, we got us a kind of situation here."

"In what way?"

"Remember I told you about that kid from Tifton named Ronnie Tibadeau, the one who fixed my heap?"

"So?"

I leaned on the car. I was thinking maybe I could just push old Ronnie's legs up under and pretend he wasn't there; drive away unnoticed. "Well, don't panic or anything," I looked down at the ever-so-still pair of legs, "but I think this is him that's dead under my car, here."

She looked for a second like it was some kind of bad joke. Then her head jabbed over to the left and down. When she was facing me again, her eyes were wide. "What have you done?"

"*Me?* I didn't do a thing."

I leaned over, took hold of the ankles, and withdrew the body whence it reposed.

Dally came slowly around the car.

I tightened my lips. "Yup. That's him all right. His head didn't used to be all stove in like that—not when I saw him last. But that's the boy. He's great with cars."

"Pull him on out."

"Love to. Take a look at his right hand."

She didn't want to, but she peeped. His right hand was handcuffed to the chassis. She straightened up. "Well, this has got to be a bit of bad news."

"I'd say so."

"What's your plan?"

"For this? I got no plan. What *can* I do? Those are *real* handcuffs. You can't pick 'em or saw 'em without a whole lot more effort than we got time for out in the open like this—in an area that's *heavily* patrolled."

Her face was pale but she tried for tough. "And what do we do about this, then, Braniac?"

I leaned over. "We sweep him under the rug right now—come back later." And I started stuffing him back under the car.

She didn't watch. "This is so very much not good."

"Yeah. And it's not even *your* car."

She was not remotely amused. "Well, hurry up." And she headed for the club.

I watched her walk away. "Be right there."

I stayed behind to tidy up. Kind of a mistake, in retrospect.

28

Ronnie's Pals

I got down on my hands and knees, always a bad
idea in any circumstance, and started shoving parts
of Ronnie up under the car. I was not happy to hear
voices coming my way, and less so when two big old
boys stopped to pass the time of night.

"Whatcha got there, mister?"

I tried to block the view. "Just fixing a little mechanical problem with the old auto."

"I don' think so."

"Really?" I craned my neck to see them.

They were fat like wrestlers, packed tight. One
was in a tank top far as I could tell in the bad light,
and the other was in a kind of sharkskin suit. The
suit was talking. "Who's that you're playin' with
down there?"

"He's my mechanic."

Tank Top shook his head. "Naw it ain't. Thas'
Ronnie Tibadeau. Or used to be, rather."

Great. "You boys know Ronnie?"

Suit smiled. "Somebody sent us over. Said he was in trouble. Looks like it was a little more than he could handle."

Tank Top: "But we're big boys." Big smile to match. "And we're used to trouble."

I straightened up. "Look, guys—he was like this when I got here."

Suit didn't buy. "Uh-huh."

Tank Top took a step closer.

I put my hand on the car door handle with a rushing sense of déjà vu. "Honest, boys. Somebody else put Ronnie up under there. Me and him, we're pals, see?" Big smile back.

No dice. Tank Top headed my way. "Sure."

I whipped open the car door. It'd worked before.

Tank Top heaved up his enormous leg, kicked my car door toward me with a boot big enough to have dinner off of—which might have been his plan for me anyway. The car door made a noise like a battleship going down, and hit me hard over nine tenths of my body. I flew east, then dropped south, all the way to the ground. Suit had somehow levitated to my side and was kicking me in the ribs with some kind of pointy Beatle-boot-looking numbers. Tank Top was laughing hard. All I could do was roll.

After a minute or so they got tired, and I sat up. "Okay. What now?"

Suit had to think. "We tie you up to Ronnie Tibadeau and go for a little drive?"

I shook my head. "Oh, let's not. Ronnie's had a pretty hard day, from the look of it." I tried to stand up, but I couldn't remember how.

Tank Top had an idea. "Let's just take him back to the man and go. I got a party."

I had to ask. "The *man*?"

Tank Top didn't mind answering. "Told us where to find you."

Who'd have known where to find me?

They hoisted me up and started me off down the street. I wasn't much help. I couldn't remember how to walk either.

It was an uneventful stroll under the streetlamps. We turned in at a darkened bed-and-breakfast, up the walk, around the porch to a side entrance, and into a small backroom. It was quite well appointed. I threw myself into a very nice Queen Anne.

But the *man* wasn't there—the guy who'd set these two tops spinning my way. Suit was only mildly irritated, but Tank Top seemed downright uncomfortable.

"I ain't waitin' for him. I gotta go, man. I need a little *help*. You see what I mean."

Anybody who'd ever seen a junkie without a bag would have known what he meant.

Suit was less than sympathetic. "Your own fault, bud. You need to be clean like me."

"I need to be clean like your *mother*."

Suit spoke calmly. "If you talk about our mother that way, I have to *cut* you, so shut up, okay? It's disrespectful." Then he approached me. "Our host, he's not in at the moment."

I tried. "So who *is* our host?"

"Our host must remain . . . anonymous."

For one icy second I had a shot of the *big* fear. The dark forces collided and extinguished every bit of light. I suddenly was afraid that our host was the guy named Lenny that I used to know. I may have mentioned him once or twice—and he was still out there in the darkness . . . somewhere.

I tried to sound cool. "Is it Lenny?"

He was clearly ignorant. "Who?"

"Well, that's a relief." You just don't know.

"The guy that sent us on our little errand is a bad man. He straddles good and evil."

Tank Top had recovered enough to respond. "I hate that kinda talk." He looked right at me. "He reads all these books and it makes him talk . . . funny."

In another light I suppose it could have been a little humorous. So I made bold to ask. "What are you reading?"

"Right now?" Suit put on his thinking cap—to all appearances a seldom-used accessory—and found the answer. "It's about two sisters."

Tank Top was suddenly all kid. "Tell it again."

Without a second of hesitation, like a hood relating the details of a caper, Suit began to tell me and his bro a tale about two sisters and a magic doll.

29

The Magic Doll

And Suit's story went as follows:

In a little village by the sea, not so very long ago, there lived two sisters. Their father was a rich sea captain, but his ship had been lost, with all hands, in Baffin Bay, where the whale fishes blow. When they heard this terrible news, the two girls began to grow in a contrary manner. As one grew bright as the sun, so sad as winter grew the other. Veronica became more graceful with each passing day. Susan was filled sorrow.

Now, on the southern-most end of this same coast, in a dense forest never visited by townsfolk or sailors, there lived the mighty witch that everyone called the Sea Hag. She was two hundred years old and had practiced her profession for most of her life. It was widely known that she ate lightning for dinner, and that her snoring could be heard as thunder on a stormy night. She was nearly six feet tall, but so stooped and twisted that her chin nearly scraped the floor when she walked. Her laughter was the sound of peacocks screaming.

So, in the dark and rainy season, in the autumn of the year, there came up a strong wind. It blew all the candles in the house out. On that night Blackeyed Susan grabbed her sister by the arm. "Look what's happened. All the candles have gone out. What will we do? We'll never have light in this house again. It's dark as the grave."

Veronica strained to see in the darkness. "Can't we just relight the candles?"

Susan was terrified. "No! That would bring down the wrath of the Sea Hag on this house!"

Veronica shivered. "The Sea Hag? What's she got to do with it?"

Susan squinted in the dim room. "She's the mistress of the darkness. Once you've let all the light in your house go out, you have to consult the Sea Hag and beg her for light. If you don't, her revenge will be swift and terrible. She'll burn your house. She'll char your bones. She'll fill your land with salt water. And it's all our fault. Imagine what Father would say! You *have* to go to the Sea Hag and beg her to let us have more light."

Veronica was terrified. The girls had heard the tales of the Sea Hag all their lives, and knew that no one who had gone in search of her had ever returned. With their father gone to sea, they had no one to turn to in their bitter hour—except the one thing Veronica's father had given her before he left: a tiny wooden doll. The doll was as beautiful as it was strange, and Veronica had always had a feeling of closeness to the doll that she could not explain.

So, that dark night, sobbing, armed only with the doll, the young girl felt her way out of the house and through forbidding undergrowth into the black forest, toward the home of the Sea Hag.

And as she went, she told her troubles to the little doll. "I'm very frightened, and I know I may never see my home or my father or my sister again."

Much to her amazement, for it had never done so before, the doll spoke back. "Do not fear. Keep me hidden away safe in your pocket and no harm will come to you. I will help."

Encouraged by the brave words, Veronica pushed on in her journey all the next day until she came to a clearing, and there it was: the fabled home of the Sea Hag.

Suddenly there was a great swooping noise like a giant bat, and in rode the Sea Hag. "I thought I smelled the blood of a human." She sniffed. "Come out now or I'll char your bones!"

Trembling like a leaf, Veronica stepped out of the shadows.

The Sea Hag grinned, toothless and without mercy. "Ah, a little girl. Come in, child. Come in. You're too skinny to eat, and besides, I've just had a stingray stew. . . . I think I'll go to bed now and eat you when I wake up. Unless . . ."

Veronica summoned all her courage. ". . . unless *what*?"

The witch was quick to answer. "Sweep and clean my house so it shines like the moon, and prepare me a meal before I awake, and *maybe* I won't eat you."

Veronica's courage grew. "I'm no stranger to hard work. This sounds easy."

Angered, the Sea Hag lashed out. "Then in addition: Out on the beach there are over one hundred great fish that I've scared ashore. Gather them up, clean them all, and cook them down—and I may let you live another day."

So saying, the witch went to bed, leaving the poor girl staring toward the beach.

In despair, Veronica poured out her predicament to the doll. "I'll never be able to do all this work before she wakes up."

"Never fear," said the doll. "Lie you down and rest. I'll do the work."

Exhausted from fear and her long journey, the girl fell into an eerie, deep slumber. When she awoke the next dawn, she found that her little companion had done every one of the tasks the Sea Hag had commanded: The house was swept, the meal was cooked, and all the fish were prepared.

The girl jumped up, kissed the magic doll, tucked it safely into her pocket, and stood beside the table where the witch's meal was set. Veronica was bright as a new penny.

The Sea Hag lumbered into the room. "Is everything done?" She cast her cloudy eye about the place. "What? Not a speck of dust and all these fish cooked down?" The Hag squinted. "Well, I won't eat you today. I've got evil work to do. I'll be away from the house all day. But when I come back, you must have done an even harder task than the one you seem to have accomplished already."

Veronica only smiled. "I'm equal to any task."

The Hag nodded. "Is that so? In the back of the house there are fifty barrels of corn that I've stolen from farmers. Grind it all, and have the meal piled neatly, and use some to make my corn bread—and I *might* not use your bones to mend my fence!"

So saying, the Sea Hag swallowed her morning meal in one gulp and lifted off the ground and out the window without another word.

Once again, Veronica consulted her wooden companion. "Shall I begin to grind the corn?"

The doll whispered, "No. I will do the work."

Veronica stared at her helpmate. "Who are you? *What* are you?"

The magic doll's voice rose in the dusty air. "I am the power of strangeness. You must never be without me. But you must wait and watch for the time when *you* do the work for yourself. Now, go out and watch the sea."

So Veronica went to the edge of the sea—which she loved—and watched the waves rise and fall, as if in a hypnotic trance.

Just as the spell of the sunset on the sea was broken, the Sea Hag swooped in over her head and plowed into the sand just beside her.

"Daydreaming? Well, let's see how much of my work you've done."

Veronica ran ahead of the witch, threw open the door, and grabbed the magic doll just before the Hag came in behind her.

There, neatly in the corner, were the bags of cornmeal. And still steaming on the table was a lovely golden corn-bread cake.

The Hag swirled around the room and then

leered weirdly at Veronica. "Girl, you vex me! I've given you tasks *no* human could perform, and you've done them."

Veronica smiled. "Any task is easy when your heart is light."

The Hag looked away. "I wouldn't know about that. But I have one final test that *no* one has ever passed. It is a task you must accomplish while I am here in the room with you."

Veronica suddenly clenched the wooden doll. How could she use its wondrous power with the Sea Hag watching? Then she remembered the doll's words—she must face *this* task alone. She took in a very deep breath. "What is the final task?"

The Sea Hag grinned. It was a hideous sight, black teeth, green tongue, cracked blue lips. "You must *kiss* me!"

Veronica saw the sorrow and the pain on the face of the witch, and suddenly felt such sympathy and loving kindness that she was drawn to the old woman. She threw her arms around the withered neck and kissed the Sea Hag—not once, nor even twice, but three times, and so gently that a salty tear formed in the corner of the sad old woman's eye. Suddenly the whole room was filled with a kind of golden light. The last light of the day, perhaps. For the first time in one hundred years the Sea Hag drew herself to her full height—and smiled serenely.

The old face seemed to grow younger and stronger, and the voice was full and clear. "Your magic is great."

Veronica stood in wonder at the transformation

of the Hag, still clutching the wooden doll. "I have no magic—none of my own."

The Hag nodded. "Why did you come here? Tell me now."

Veronica answered right away, without a hint of fear. "My sister is filled with sorrow and I caused all the light in our house to go out. I had to come and get permission from you to have more light in our house."

The Hag's voice was very gentle. "I see. I see very well. You're a brave young girl. I'll give you the light you need."

So saying, the Hag went into the yard, beckoning Veronica to follow. The moon was rising. "I know all about your beautiful, strange doll. I tell you now that the doll had a life all its own, and can bring light back into your lives." The hag's voice rose. "Now go—and never come back!"

Not having to be told twice, Veronica left quickly. She had only gone a short way down the path when she turned to take one last look back—but all she saw was a little cottage in the woods and a fat old farmer's wife planting lilies in the moonlight.

Just as daylight was breaking, she came back to her own home.

When she opened the door, she was startled by Blackeyed Susan's greeting. Instead of her usual sighs and her ordinary tears, Susan was shivering with terror. "Oh, sister, sister—I'm so glad you're home. This house has had no light in it since you've been gone. No candle would stay lit . . . even the lamps borrowed from the neighbors sputtered out the instant I brought them into this place. We truly *have* been cursed by the Sea Hag!"

Veronica could only hold up the magic doll and say, "Well, I've been told that this will help."

Susan clutched the doll. "Is it magic? Will it make light?"

Suddenly a great flame, like lightning, blazed out from the doll's eye sockets. With a terrible cry of pain Susan was engulfed in light. Veronica could only watch in horror—until she realized what was truly happening.

All the pain, all the sorrow, all the tears—all were burned out of Susan's spirit. Veronica could see these dark emotions, shadow-demons, rising from her sister like smoke. In a final blinding flash Susan was caressed by a glowing peace so tangible and obvious that it could be seen on the girl's face for all to read.

Stunned, Susan sat down in the doorway of their house.

Before she could think what to do, Veronica heard the voice of the magic doll once more. "Now I'll scour these seven seas. I mean to bring your father home to you, be he in this world or in the next. You have my vow, he shall be home by spring!"

Veronica could hardly believe her ears. "But my father's gone, with all hands. I fear he's beyond returning."

The doll seemed to laugh. "Not to me. I can bring him back from wher*ever* he's gone."

With that the doll flew across the waves and disappeared.

From that day on the two sisters grew to be so alike in their performance of great deeds of loving kindness that they were often mistaken for twins. And every day, after the chores were done and the candles were lit and the sun was sinking low over the ocean's horizon, they'd go out on the beach to sit and watch the sea, arm in arm, waiting for their father to come home.

30

The Tarnished Code

My head was clearing and my ribs were really beginning to hurt. "What in the name of God would provoke you to tell me such a story?"

Suit shrugged like a man with a secret. "I've got mojo. You've got some too. I know that. What you *don't* have at the moment is a magic doll. And that's what you want. Maybe you've heard my story before."

These boys were as weird as they wanted to be, and then some. But I had to keep straight. "Yeah. I heard it before, only in the one I know, neither sister is that sad, and one of them loses her voice."

Suit almost seemed to understand what I was talking about. He squinted. "Yeah, but I'm telling you the story from *my* world. Plus, you don't know who's *got* the magic doll."

I nodded. "Okay. Now tell me the one about the guy who told you to come and find me by my car."

Tank Top was all of a sudden sad. "You should'na hurt Ronnie."

Big silence.

I tried again. "So, you're just going to let your strange little story hang in the air like this? You're not going to tell me who hired you to come get me? But, see, it's probably *that* guy that killed our pal Ronnie."

Suit shrugged. "I guess."

Tank Top sat up, inclined his head to Suit. "He don' like Ronnie that much. Thinks he's a redneck."

Suit had little patience. "He *was* a redneck. Now he's roadkill."

Tank Top was given pause. "Oh. Yeah." He seemed genuinely sorry. "Too bad. Ronnie was fun to hang with."

I chimed in. "Plus, he was great on cars. Fixed up my old heap good."

Tank Top agreed. "It was his gift. Too bad me an' him got mixed up with all this drug crap. We coulda opened up, like, a garage of somethin'."

Suit sneered. "What would *you* have done? Lift up the cars so's he could work?"

Tank Top squinted. "I was the brains of the organization."

I tried to steer the conversation back to matters more germane. "So, what now? The boss is gone. Maybe I could just be on my merry way."

Suit was not amused. "No no no. We have to keep you here. The man, he has plans for you. By and by, some cop on patrol will find Ronnie. Then we shove you at the cops so hard, you'll fall right into jail."

Tank Top was clever, all smiles. "Do not pass *Go*, do not collect—"

Suit kept it short. "Shut up." He looked at me. "My brother, in case you have not already gathered up this information on your very own, is an idiot."

I sat back. "You all don't look that much alike for brothers."

Both nodded, then, together: "Thanks."

Smiles all around.

Tank Top, all other grievances forgotten, clarified it for me. "It's good to work with the family."

I nodded.

Tank Top looked at his brother then, with more than a little urgency. "No kiddin'. I'm in a bad way."

Heavy sigh. "All right." Suit shot me a look. "You got any ideas that I can't take care of you myself if my brother goes off to wreck his health?"

I was clear. "None whatsoever."

Tank Top stood. He put out his big hand to me. We shook. He was very respectful. "Well, bud, I guess that's it. I'm goin' to a party, you goin' to jail. Life's like that sometimes."

I finally got a clear look at him. "Hey." Boy, did he look familiar. Could it have been? "Did I see you out on the beach earlier, maybe following me and my friend up to The Hut?"

He was suddenly sharp. "Anything can happen." Stumbled to the door, turned around, waved at us both. "Never can tell." And he was gone, out the door, melted into the muggy night.

Suit watched after him. "He is an idiot. But, you know, he is also my brother."

"Right."

He eyeballed me to beat the band. "You've got no

chance to mess with me. I'd kill you just like I'd gut a fish."

Hmm. Gut a fish. I don't know why, but I was thinking of Lydia all of a sudden. I looked around the room. Things were in a fair state of disarray. "Looks like you all already had a party in here."

He shrugged. "It was like this when we got here."

I craned my neck. "Blood in the bathroom."

He didn't care. "That's the room for it."

"Could be Ronnie's blood, you know."

"None of my business. Ronnie and I were not that close. He was a runner for some of our associates. Dumb as a melon. Had a habit. I've got no respect for a man with a habit."

"Unless he's your brother."

"My brother is my business."

I decided to take a different tack. "Family, huh?"

Worked. He softened. "What can you do?"

I was getting a stronger feeling of Lydia. It was very weird. Was that her blood there in the bathroom?

"I've got to go to the bathroom."

"No, you don't."

"I swear, I'd know if I had to go. I think you kicked something loose in here."

He remembered. "Oh, yeah. It was probably the kidneys."

"Yeah."

"Okay."

I lumbered up, made it to the bathroom. It was a mess. There was blood and hair on the sink and everything was in disarray. I got a good gander at the layout before I went back into the other room.

"Kind of a mess in there."

He shrugged. What did he care. Wasn't his place.

What I couldn't help noticing was a woman's umbrella on the floor by the bed.

I inclined by head toward it. "Whose umbrella?"

He looked. "I dunno."

"Belongs to a lady."

"Or a sissy boy."

"Uh-huh. Was the boss here for fun or business?"

He considered. "Far as I could tell, the guy was all business."

"So the lady, if there was one, was not entertainment."

"Not likely—but not impossible."

"You're pretty free with the opinions."

"What do I care?" Big smile.

Why was he so amiable?

"So we're pals now?"

"Well, as it happens, Mr. Tucker—for all my faults—I'm something of a fan of yours."

"How would you even know who I am?"

"You've got a reputation."

"No, I don't."

"You don't have to like it, but you have to know there's some people that know who you are."

"Hey, *I* don't even know who I am half the time."

"Whatever."

"No kidding. How do you know who I am?"

"Okay, I've been told."

"By?"

He was sly. "Got my sources."

I was suddenly feeling very paranoid. "Sources."

He decided to let me off the hook. "I told you. I know Ronnie. You cipher it out."

"Ronnie said something nice about me."

"He thought you were a great man, he said."

"So why'd I kill him, then?"

Suit was very philosophical. "I don't expect you did, after all." He lowered his voice. "Those were police handcuffs on him, looked like to me."

Ronnie worked for Lowe and Tommy. Tommy was a cop. You cipher it out. Two and two really do, sometimes, make four. What do you know?

That told me what I thought I needed to know, so I decided to play my ace. It's an old trick. I'd used it recently without meaning to. I started breathing.

You breathe in, you breathe out—by and by, you get into quite a trance.

He was nervous. "Hey. What are you doin'?"

I had my eyes open, but they were glazed.

Suit sidled over. "Cut it out, bud."

I was in another reality. I was in the center of the breath.

He shook me. "Hey. Hey. You're not *dying* on me, man. Damn!"

And he started shaking me all over town. Now, ordinarily a young tough such as our boy in the fine suit would be more than a match for yours truly. But as it was, he was distracted by his own mind, and I had an unfair advantage, which I used almost immediately.

I popped out my arm right into his solar plexus. The bones did the work. He didn't stand a chance. He was hit with several feet of solid bone in a delicate portion of his guts.

Surprised, he took a step back. I popped him one

in the nuts. Sorry, but when you're a layabout like me, you have to take every opportunity.

He had something to say about it all in some other language. He fell on his backside.

I refrained from kicking him like he had me, but I got over to him quick so he'd know exactly how much business I meant.

Right away he understood. "Okay. Okay. I can see you might be mad, but it's just a job for me. It don't mean a thing."

Just in case, he was covering up.

I spared him. But I had questions. "Who sent you after me?"

He groaned. "You know I can't tell you that."

"And I suppose a little soccer practice on your head bone wouldn't loosen up your moral objections?"

He managed to sit halfway up. "Look . . . Flap . . . I've got absolutely nothing against you. Like I said, I'm a fan—and I think we have something special in common, if you see what I mean. Plus, you took care of Pevus Arnold, and that's okay by me, if I do say so—given the circumstances and all. But I've got a code. You can kick all the stuffing out of me that you want to, the code don't change." He leaned back against the footboard of the bed and eased his troubled guts. "But let me also say, and just see if this sounds familiar: 'If you started something, you'd have to kill me. I wouldn't quit coming till you did. You can take that to the bank,' or words to that effect."

Words to that effect, nothing. It was an exact quote. It only took me a second to make the connection. It was a final confirmation.

I looked down at him. "So. What, exactly, do you and I do now?"

He relaxed. I wasn't going to kick him. He could see that. "You go your way and I go mine? No point, no foul. You and me could skuffle about like this back an' forth all night long if we wanted, but I've got to go and worry about my bro—and I expect you've got troubles enough of your own too. I don't want to pop you, you don't want to pop me. Let's let it go at that."

"*Que sera, sera.*"

He tried getting to his feet. "I *love* Doris Day."

I took his elbow and helped him up.

He straightened himself out. "What was that thing you were doing. I thought you'd had a heart attack. You looked, like, *dead.*"

"It's all breath. Breath and concentration."

"Ohhh." But he didn't see.

"So can I really rely on your not following me anymore?"

He considered. "Look. My job was: I find you and bring you here. Can we agree I've done that?"

"Done and done."

"So . . ."

". . . according to the code . . ."

". . . my work here is finished."

I had to smile. "Guy's *got* to have a code."

He agreed. "Without it we are little more than rude animals."

"Amen."

He looked at me. "Just a word of advice: our so-called host with the handcuffs? He's nuts and tough all at the same time. He's got some kinda bad Jones.

Not a drug, I don't guess. But it's something heavy that motivates the man—so, you know, watch your butt."

"Words to live by."

He blinked, fussed with his tie, nodded a farewell. "I make it a part of *my* code."

And he was gone.

21

Little Shadows

I beat it back to the car, taking notes about the location of the bed-and-breakfast as I went. Poor old Ronnie was lying undisturbed right where we had left him. I hustled myself on down to River Street.

Dally was in the dark in the front of the joint; zipped the door open when she saw me coming.

"Where the hell have you been?"

"Took a little longer to take care of Ronnie. I met up with some of his pals."

She got closer. "What?"

"Not now. I got a really bad feeling about something. But I gotta ask the boys here a few key questions so I'll know which way is up."

She kept the lights in front off, and got a nice booth in the back. Called out to the Turners. "Boys? Y'all come on in here, okay?"

They wandered in like they'd just gotten out of high school gym.

Maytag smiled. "Hey, Mr. Tucker. Where you been?"

"Out. Mind if we chat?"

He was agreeable. "What's on your mind?"

Peachy sat too.

I stood. "Whatever else is on my mind, I got a few pressing questions."

Maytag nodded. "Such as?"

"You all got away from the cops fairly well back on the island. I didn't even know they were outside."

Maytag grinned. "Shoot. We heard 'em comin' halfway up the path."

Peachy added. "What in the world you think we were doin' goin' to bed so early?"

Dally had to rib me. "You're some detective. They heard the cops comin', and you called me for a chat."

Maytag tried to help me out. "It's our years of huntin'. We hear the sounds of the forest. We knew it was men comin' up. Then we escaped silently and"— he looked around mysteriously—"we blended with the shadows."

Peachy nodded.

Maytag went on. "Besides, we did what we wanted: got you to help us find Lydia."

Peachy spoke up to me. "You think she'll come back there?"

I nodded. "To the graveyard? Yes, I do."

He wanted to know. "How come?"

Dally interrupted. "He's got a system. Don't ask about it, but it works. It's kinda like a hunch."

"Ohhh." The twins nodded slowly, in unison.

I wasn't finished. "So you just left me there."

Peachy smiled. "Shoot. We let you get rescued from us evil kidnappers."

Maytag shoved in. "Saved by the hometown brigade."

Peachy tapped his brother. "That's right. What's that boy they say plays a fiddle?"

I had the answer. "Taylor. Plays the viola."

Again with the unison "Ohhh."

Peachy began to philosophize. "He's a good boy, seems like to me. He don't wanna be no policeman. He wants to be a musician." He took a breath. "Did you ever think how much damage is done in this world by people that hates their jobs?"

Maytag offered. "Like those postal workers you always hear about."

It made me nervous to think that in my reflective moments I examined the same mysteries of the universe that plagued the Turner twins.

Dally saved me from my reverie. "You boys knocked us out good. Your daddy's sleeping pills are still working on me."

Peachy was concerned. "You still sleepy, Ms. Oglethorpe?"

"Not sleepy. They got me kinda . . . jumpy."

Maytag nodded. "It's the aftereffects."

Dally went on. "Yeah, but what I mean is, how come you didn't just motor on up to our table at The Hut, have a seat, and ask Flap to help you find Lydia?"

"You was bein' followed."

She looked at me.

I confirmed. "Savannah cops had a tail on us. Our friend Ronnie Tibadeau was involved. I thought

I saw somebody weird on the beach, but I was preoccupied." She took a breath, but I wouldn't let her get to her point. "And Detective Acree already made fun of me for missing the tail, so you can skip the wisecracks."

She went back to Maytag. "So you saw a guy tailin' us?"

"Uh-huh. We knew you was bein' watched, so we had to get away where we could talk a little while. I was personally hopin' it would be longer, but, like we say, the police come in on us."

Dally squinted. "So how come the cops didn't see you two cartin' me an' Flap out of The Hut?"

Maytag shrugged, very calm. "Like I said, we blend with the shadows."

Very mysterious, if it's possible to be mysterious and goofy at the same time.

Dally pressed. "You had more you wanted to tell Flap?"

"Maybe."

"You want to talk now?"

I settled back in my seat. "You want to tell me exactly what happened the day of the murder?"

He nodded. Peachy looked around, once again checking to see that nobody was lurking outside.

Dally sat back. "Okay. Let's hear it."

Maytag began his story.

32

Murder

The day of the murder was hot and bright. About ten in the morning the twins showed up at the bank, summoned by Lowe Acree. It was full of people. Maytag, because he was the older of the boys, had determined he would do all the talking.

They sidled up to the desk out front of Lowe's office. Connie greeted them.

"Hey, boys. Mr. Acree is expecting you." She lowered her voice. "He's in a worse mood than usual. You all be careful what you say."

Peachy couldn't resist a few words. "Maytag's gonna do all the talkin'."

She smiled.

They went into Lowe's office. Lowe was indeed in a rare mood.

"Well. The Ton of Twins." He was simultaneously making fun of the way they pronounced their last name and their size. He thought he was very clever.

The boys smiled. Peachy waved.

Maytag talked. "We got your message."

Lowe cracked his knuckles. "So. You know it won't do any good to mess with me. I mean business. You sell me that land, I don't cause you any trouble. I pay a fair price. Otherwise your daddy's loans and mortgages and anything else I can scare up, they all be in a wad of trouble so thick he won't be able to buy a peanut to boil. I can mess you all up so bad you won't ever get out from under. Your great-great-grandbabies—if you all are capable of reproducing—will *still* be in complete financial ruin far past the next century."

Maytag sat down in one of the chairs in front of Lowe's desk and motioned Peachy to sit in the other. They sat in silence.

The silence made Lowe madder. "So what's it going to be, boys? You jack-leg retards wanna ruin your family for the next two hundred years?"

Maytag appeared to think about it. "No. No, sir, I don't believe we'd like to do that."

"That's right. So you sell me that land, and everything is fine. You get a little extra play money, and I get a piece of land you don't use anyway. Everybody's happy."

Maytag tried to choose his words carefully. "That land—is made to grow pines and things, and keep deer on. And to produce blackberries. And to maybe clear one day and sell the timber and build a house for the grandbabies you expressed a concern for, which was nice of you. That land is not for a Dempster Dumpster. It ain't no garbage can. I can't live with the idea that you'd put poison down in it, just because you got nowhere else to get rid of it. Can you see the difference? One way the land is alive, and the other way the land is dead. And I can't be responsible for killin' it." That was the end of his speech.

Lowe lurched forward. "You feeble dickweed retard. You got absolutely no idea what I want to use that land for."

Maytag was calm. "Chemical dump."

"Shut up. You're too stupid to understand my business. All I have to do is put some kind of a lien on the property against whatever your daddy owes, or what I can make up, and I could get the land anyway. I'm trying to do you a favor."

"We appreciate that."

Lowe just got madder. He stood up. "I'm going to have that piece of crap acreage whether you sell it to me or not."

"Now, see . . . that's just the problem, Mr. Acree. You think of it as a piece of crap, and we think of it—"

"Shut up! You're too stupid to think of it as anything! I'll mess you all up so bad, you won't be able to sleep at night."

"I never yet had any trouble sleepin'—"

"I said to shut up! You got no idea what trouble is. I got money. I got reputation. I got the law in my pocket. You got dick!"

Without any kind of warning Lydia Habersham Acree slipped into the room. She'd apparently been in Lowe's private bathroom. She'd been crying, and one side of her face looked bright red, like it was sunburned or sore.

"Lowe, sit down."

He whipped around to face her. "I'm not finished with you either. You just go back in there and wait till I'm done with my business."

"No, Lowe. I'm not staying."

He got from around his desk and started for her. "Oh, yes you are."

Maytag was up in a flash, bumped him like a football player blocking. Lowe took a tumble against his back wall. Peachy was up on the other side of him, and the twins gently locked his arms at his side. Just as Lowe started to holler, Maytag got him in a kind of choke hold, and Lowe couldn't even breathe. Yelling was out of the question.

They wrestled him back to his seat.

Peachy whispered into Maytag's ear. "I know I ain't supposed to talk here, but if you don't let go of this man's throat, he'll pass out."

Maytag whispered back. "That's what I want him to do. Then he'll be quiet. Besides, it ain't his throat, it's his jugulars that counts."

Peachy made a face. "Don't do it too long."

He didn't. Lydia was helping them get Lowe to his chair. She leaned over to Lowe and whispered in his ear.

All they could hear was the first part: "You've struck me for the third and final time."

And then Lowe fell forward onto the desk, and his forehead hit with a very loud whack.

Lydia was crying, and the boys saw blood trickling out from underneath Lowe's head. Maytag pointed Lydia back into the bathroom. She went. Peachy leaned over to check Lowe's breathing. It was shallow, but there.

He hollered out, "Connie, come in here quick. Somethin's the matter with Lowe."

She came in, panicked, called the ambulance, the police, and the fire department. Everybody in the bank was at the door. Maytag checked the bathroom, but Lydia had somehow vanished.

With a glance the twins saw a chance to leave quietly, too, while all the attention was on Lowe. They left, went by Lydia's house. Her car was gone. They went home, told their father what had happened. He tried to get them to stay and find out what had happened to Lowe, but they were worried about Lydia, and took off.

They found out on the radio news, later that evening on their drive south, that Lowe was dead; they were wanted. They'd been looking for Lydia ever since. When they couldn't find her, they'd called their father, and he'd told them about me.

That's when they came to me for help.

22

Lydia in Autumn

That was the story.

Dally was straight. "So maybe you did kill him."

Maytag laughed out loud. "Shoot. I squeezed Ida harder than that, and she's a old woman."

Peachy wasn't laughing. "Lydia whispered a thing into him, like in the story. That's what made him die."

Maytag hushed his brother.

We sat for a minute, but it got to Dally. "Story? Sounds like the one Sally told me."

Peachy looked at Maytag. Maytag nodded. Peachy looked back at Dally. "See, we given her a book for Christmas. It was just after that Thanksgivin' pageant."

Maytag couldn't help himself. He had to tell me. "We taken first prize in the giant pumpkin."

Peachy was sidetracked. "Big as a Ford truck engine."

Maytag nodded. "Maybe bigger."

Peachy was lost in reminiscence. "And we took to

Lydia right away. She stood in front of that pumpkin just a-starin' at it and sayin' how that big round face reminded her of a harvest moon."

Maytag smiled, remembering too. "We carved a human face out of it the second day after we won the prize."

Peachy went on. "Anyways, we got to talkin' in the cool autumn air—I love the fall. She was so sweet, and that pretty hair—I tell you what's the truth, I had me a crush on 'er right then and there."

Maytag patted his brother's arm. "It happened thataway with Momma and Daddy: met at a fair, liked each other right away."

Peachy shook his head. "We got to know her. Lots of people was scared of her, how strange she was. But we . . ."

Maytag helped. "We never had no little sister. That's what it was."

Peachy grinned right at me. "Crush wore off. She's just too crazy for a girlfriend."

Maytag agreed. "But, with everything about our family, you know, we thought she'd fit right in as a member. We got us a whole buncha crazy kin. And when you meet her, you can tell . . . there's somethin' not right about her."

Peachy muscled in. "Anyway, she was always talkin' about how much she loved bein' out on the sea. She said it was clean and the waves made her forget. Didn't never say what there was to forget. So, but—we got her a book of stories about it."

Maytag detailed. "*Folktales of the Southern Sea Islands.*"

Peachy was proud. "She loved it. Read it over and over."

Maytag nodded. "Seemed to have a right strong effect on her."

Peachy turned to me again. "Because, like we said, she ain't . . ." But he couldn't find the words exactly.

I explained it to Dally. "The boys think Lydia's not human."

Dally was very dry. "Maybe she's not."

I had to toss her a look. "What would you know about it, missy?"

"Missy?"

"You heard me."

She looked away. "Save it."

That was it. She knew something about Lydia that she wasn't telling me, but I wouldn't get another peep out of her on the subject. I knew better. So I went back to the twins. "How'd you get off the is- land? There were guards at the boats. I saw them when Taylor, the viola-boy, took me home."

"We had a boat on the other end under some bushes."

Peachy finished. "Just in case."

I summed up. "You guys heard the cops coming from half a mile off, sneaked out unseen in the last of daylight, made it to the other end of the island where you had stashed an extra boat for just such an emer- gency, got back to Savannah, figured I'd go to the Old Old Baptist, and found me there."

They nodded their famous unison nod.

Dally shoved a look my way. "Why would they figure that?"

I raised my eyebrows. "They know I like a good story."

Maytag nodded. "Yep."

I looked at Dally. "That's where the angel is—the angel that took Ida's voice away. They had to know that's where I'd go. That statue marks a pivotal point in their lives even long before they were born. That's the place that altered their mother and their aunt. Visiting it's like a pilgrimage. They had to go there. They had to know I'd be curious enough to go there myself. It's too big a deal."

Dally nodded, but I wasn't certain she understood.

I looked back at the boys. "You're *not* stupid. But you *could* be guilty. It's good guilty murder-planning stealth you all exhibited."

Peachy shrugged. "Or we could just know how the police are."

Maytag continued. "Especially Tommy Acree."

Peachy: "He don't like us."

Maytag: "For some reason."

They sat like bumps on a log, and I use the phrase advisedly. I began to think; always a danger sign. Either they were the simplest boys in town, or they were nothing like what they seemed, and very devious—and very dangerous. One way they were clever, cold killers. The other way they were the lilies of the field. It was a wide berth, and I'd been fooled before by people who seemed sweet and simpleminded and had turned out to be very, very wrong. It's a great cover for a murderer.

Dally caught me. "Hey, Flap. You're thinkin'."

"Oh. Yeah. Sorry."

"Try not to let it happen again."

The boys giggled like little kids.

Dally gave them the eye stronger than usual. "You boys don't look that much alike—for twins."

They both sobered up quick. Maytag looked at Peachy. "Should we tell 'em?"

Long pause.

Peachy squinted. "I dunno. Maybe not."

Maytag nodded. "Still—it's a good story. Might be useful some kinda way for Mr. Tucker."

Peachy considered. "And Ms. Oglethorpe like her a story."

Maytag nodded. "It's a good story." He looked at me. "Wanna hear how come we don't look much like twins?"

I smiled. "I think it's got something to do with Aunt Ida."

Dally wanted to get it. "How in the world would you know a thing like that?"

I kept staring at Maytag. "Because it's one of my theories about something Aunt Ida was trying to tell me when I left her porch, right?"

He smiled right back. "You surely are a smart man." He looked at his brother. "Peach? You wanna tell it?"

Peachy took up the mantle.

24

Sisters and Mothers

As was widely known, Ida and Mavis Habersham of
Savannah, Georgia, were as close as sisters can get.
What one had, the other wanted. What one wanted,
the other tried to get. They were like one person. They
did all their work together, wore the same clothes, and
shared secrets far into the night.

As they grew, they were quite popular, and boys
dated both girls all through high school. One autumn they went with a big church group to the
county fair inland.

At the fair J. D. Tucker saw Mavis—just once,
walking down the path to the livestock area—and he
decided then and there that she was the one for him.
He was instantly struck with permanent love. Sometimes it happens. He vowed to his friends that the
only work he would do from that moment on would
be to court that girl until she married him. The farm
could go to weed, the plow could rust, the tractor

could just fall apart. It didn't matter. All that mattered was marrying Mavis.

They were wed the next spring. Ida was the maid of honor, and was just as happy as Mavis.

The next autumn, a year to the day since J.D. had first seen Mavis, they discovered she was pregnant. Ida was just as happy as Mavis.

As Mavis got closer to the time of delivering her firstborn, Ida came to stay with her and J.D. to help out around the house and to share the experience with her sister. They were like one person again. They did all their work together, wore the same clothes, and shared secrets far into the night.

J.D. was worried about his wife, and worked all the time, partly so they'd have enough money for the baby, and partly to keep himself occupied so he wouldn't sit around thinking about what might go wrong. He worked all day on the farm, all evening at a Feed and Seed, and all night as a watchman for a bank over in Tifton. He only slept five hours out of twenty-four, and even then it was a restless sleep.

One night in May there came up a thunderstorm that people still talk about to this day: hail the size of house bricks, constant lightning searing the sky as bright as noon, roaring thunder that made it impossible to hear anything else.

J.D. was at the bank when the storm began, and all the power in town went out. He tried to make some phone calls, but the phone lines were out too. He was impossibly torn between the awful worry about his wife and the imperative of staying at his job in such an emergency. He stayed at the bank, because he thought it was the right thing to do, but the bank owners didn't know that. They always thought, from that night on, that J.D. had deserted his post and gone home to his wife and sister-in-law, leaving their money unprotected. Some time after his long hours were done, and he'd headed home to his wife, the power came back on and the alarms sounded. When everybody got to the bank, of course J.D. had gone. It was nearly two hours past his quitting time. He never bothered to protest against the accusations, even when the bankers fired him. J.D. knew what he'd done, and he knew he'd done right. That was the start of a feud between the two families that has lasted into the present day.

On the night of the storm in Beautiful the sisters were scared to death. Lightning was popping the ground all around their little house, and thunder continuously rattled the windows and shook the walls. Hail broke through weak places in the roof and pounded craters in the truck outside. The kitchen garden was destroyed in the first half hour. Lightning struck the feed corn in the second hour and set it on fire, but the rain and hail were so furious that they put out the fire before it could completely burn down the crib.

Mavis was so terrified, huddled in the middle of the kitchen, that she was thrown into labor.

But so was Ida. That's the secret of the story. Ida was just as pregnant as Mavis. What one sister had, the other one always wanted.

This was the secret of all secrets the sisters had shared. When Mavis had told her sister all about the glories of married life, Ida had been jealous and wanted the same love that Mavis had. She'd found it in the arms of someone remarkable, but she never revealed the identity of her paramour. She'd become increased with child as she'd lived with her sister, but they'd kept to themselves. No one but J.D. saw them, and even though he'd had suspicions, he'd never voiced them.

Now, on this terrible night, because of the trauma of the storm, the two women delivered their babies together. Mavis had trouble. Ida didn't, even though her baby was premature.

J.D. arrived at his home in the first light of the next morning. When he saw the smoldering corn crib and the battered roof and the ruined garden, he just stood outside the house, afraid to go in.

He was only roused to cross the threshold by the sound of babies crying. He rushed into the bedroom, and there were Mavis and Ida in bed, each holding a tiny newborn.

When he came into the room, Ida woke up. Mavis didn't. She had passed away in the night while the other three had slept; while J.D. had protected the Tifton Home Loan.

He sat down on the bed and took up the child out of Mavis's arms, and cried like the day Jesus was buried.

Later he gathered up what he supposed to be his twin boys. Even though he had suspicions, he didn't make them known. He left Ida sleeping and called the Peaker Family Mortuary, Caring Since 1934. Old Mr. Peaker made all the arrangements to bury Mavis Habersham Turner in her family plot at the Old Old Baptist Church in Savannah, Georgia.

When they were in high school, the boys had come home wondering why they didn't look anything alike. They'd just had a biology lesson. At the dinner table Ida calmly tapped out the story she'd never before told to a soul and had kept all these years in her heart. Mr. Turner just stared at the food he was eating, like he always did at the dinner table. When the boys wanted to know which son belonged to Mavis and which to Ida, she said she didn't know. When they wanted to know who was the father of the other boy, she said she'd never tell—except to say it was nobody they knew. They could see she was telling the truth, and never asked about it again.

When they looked to their father for some kind of answer, he told them his opinion. "Sometimes your family ain't what you was born with. Sometimes your family is who you say it is. I say you're both my boys. That's all."

That was good enough for everybody, and they'd never worried a minute about it since. They agreed that J.D. was their father; Ida was their aunt. It was settled because they'd *decided* it was settled. It didn't take anything more than that.

35

Dream Reunion

Peachy grinned, happy to have told his tale to another living soul, happy to see the effect it had on his audience.

But I was confused. "So . . . Lydia really could be some kind of relative."

Dally shot in. "No, she couldn't—not to *them,* I don't think."

"But she's a Habersham, the mother and the aunt were Habershams. . . ."

"Flap, take my word for it. Lydia's not a Habersham."

Maytag nodded. "Took us a while to figure that one out, too, Mr. Tucker."

I looked at him. "And you really don't know which is which, who's the other father, none of it?"

They shook their heads, but they were smiling. They really didn't care. It really was settled in their minds.

Dally wouldn't let me go. "See, Flap: The event

happens, devoid of any valuation. *You* impart the meaning to it."

"Shut up."

The boys looked at her. She responded. "That's a little bit of Tucker horse manure that he's always slingin' around. He can dish it out, but he's not much in the 'takin' it' department, is he?"

Peachy grinned at me. "She got you there, Mr. Tucker."

I kept my dignity. "Shut up, the both of you. I'm still trying to get why Lydia's *not* related to you. Not to mention: How come you never told me your own mother was buried in the same graveyard where all that other business happened?"

They looked at each other. Peachy answered. "Just . . . didn't seem to fit the line of conversation at the time."

Maytag agreed. "Besides, you know about it *now*."

"I don't know anything now. I don't know who you two are. I don't know half of what Dally's talking about. I don't know who Lydia is or why we have to find her. And I don't know who killed Lowe Acree or why."

Dally patted my arm. "Finished?"

I shook my head. "I'm just getting started. And by the way"—I shot my gaze right back to the boys—"your father knew your mother less than two years and hasn't forgotten her in the last twenty-seven?"

Peachy was more serious than I'd seen him. "He loved her, Mr. Tucker. Permanently."

I wasn't sure. "Yeah, but . . ."

Dally helped. "Maybe if she'd lived, she'd be complaining about his snoring by now; he'd be grouchy about her reading in bed or somethin'—but as it is, she died while he was still in love. Nothin' can help that."

I gave up. "Okay. But the rest of it. It's making me nuts."

Dally put a cooling hand on my shoulder. "You know what you need? You need to do your little trick. You need to get right in your mind and find Lydia and solve the murder of Lowe Acree and go back home to your nice loud apartment in the city and come over to Easy and character up the place." She patted me. "That's what you need."

The boys were nodding at me. I didn't know if they understood anything about what she was saying, but they were very supportive. There was little choice involved. Dally said it was time: It was time.

"Got another room or something where I can go and have a moment to myself?"

She smiled. "How about what used to be the assistant manager's office?"

"Funny."

"Remember where it is?"

"Not even remotely."

She pointed. "Around the corner, first office on the left. We'll wait here."

I nodded. The boys smiled. Dally waved. I was up and around the corner in what seemed to me an awkward silence. Once I was in the office, I could hear that they had resumed conversation, but I couldn't hear the words at all. It was just a kind of pleasant murmur.

I sat in the only chair in the room. I tried to get everything out of my head. All the weird family histories and connections and gothic idiocies. I tried to see the golden curtain wafting in front of me. Since I didn't have the luxury of looking out at the sea, I tried to breathe like the sound of the waves. I know it sounds wacky, but it helps.

I don't know how much time went by just breathing in, breathing out, breathing in, seeing nothing. But finally it came back: the waking dream, the family reunion; everybody sitting around tables eating fried chicken. The Turners and the Acrees and Horace from Atlanta and Pevus Arnold and his wife, and all the strange inhabitants of my recent days—they were all eating fried chicken and drinking from mason jars that said *Rusty's Barbecue* on the label on the side.

And there, across the yard, was Lydia waving, her face turned away from my view. "Hello, Flap. Good to see you again." She was standing by the stone angel, laughing. The graveyard by the church was dark and filled with open graves and magnolia trees. Lowe Acree was popping up out of one of the graves. Lydia was laughing at him uncontrollably. I came over to stop her, since no one else seemed able to do it. When I got there, still with her face turned away, she said, "Hello, Flap. Good to see you again." It was like a broken record. It echoed in a kind of musical way.

I walked closer to her. I had a very strong feeling of finally scratching an itch I'd had forever. It was very satisfying. In that moment of relief I found myself right next to Lydia. In the darkness her voice sounded so familiar. She said, still keeping her face turned away from me, "You have to come tonight. It's the last night I'll be here."

I reached my hand up to brush the hair away from her face, and turned it toward me so I could finally see her clearly. It was like trying to move my hand underwater, in slow motion.

When I finally touched her, and *saw* who she was, the shock of seeing that face snapped me out of my reverie like a rifle shot through the forehead.

36

Stone Angel

I shoved myself up; scrambled around the desk and out the door. "Dally!"

"Flap? You okay?"

I rounded the corner, moving fast. She could see I wasn't okay. "We gotta get back to the churchyard now."

"What's the matter?"

I was madder at her than I think I'd ever been. "You know what's the matter."

My being mad like that, it made the boys nervous, which just poured gasoline on the fire of my suspicions about them. They had no idea what was up with me, but they could see it wasn't good. Nobody made a peep. They could see it would set me off. They could see nobody would want to set me off in the shape I was in. It could have international repercussions. We just gathered ourselves up and zipped like hornets out the door.

We must have been a sight, the four of us, God

knows what hour of the night, traipsing up from the river and on toward the cemetery. We were four silhouettes from two different worlds: two urban swells, two simple farm boys. Or two suckers and two killers, that was a possibility too.

And what do you know: It actually is darkest just before the dawn. The night was late, moon was set, and outside the protection of the streetlights it was black as the belly of the beast.

We slouched into the boneyard like grave robbers, looking every direction at once. I was in the lead, strong and holy from the vision I'd had. Okay, maybe the magic didn't always work like this, but it was powerful and terrifying when it did.

I headed straight for the stone angel where Ida had left her voice so many years before. Somewhere close, the remains of somebody's mother lay resting. And not far away was the last earthly evidence of strangers who gave their lives in the Revolutionary War so that we would all have the inalienable right to mispronounce English in America.

There was somebody already standing by the angel. She was in a white, airy summer dress, and in the thick, humid night anybody would have put her down as a ghost. The others hung back, unsure of what was going down. They stayed in the shadows. I, only, am escaped, alone, to tell thee. I approached the apparition.

She was staring at the angel so intently, I thought it might bust. It seemed more glowing than before. I walked heavily to announce my presence, but she was undistracted. I sidled up next to her. She knew I was there. We just stood, the both of us, looking at the angel.

Finally she looked my way, calmly. "Hello, Flap. Good to see you again."

"Hello, Lydia." Only the name wasn't Lydia when I knew her before. She used to be called Sylvia. Cousin Sylvia.

27

Cousins, No Kissing

I might not have recognized her if I hadn't met her first in the dream thing. It had been quite a long time since I'd last seen her. But all kinds of things were coming back to me. I was remembering how my cousin Sylvia was something of a *very* free spirit, even in the young days. She used to tell everybody she was from another planet. Lots of people believed her.

When she was in the third grade, she made up her own language—a complete language with its own rules of diction, grammar—everything. The last time I'd seen her was when the family visited her in the state mental hospital in Milledgeville. She wasn't nuts, she was just very smart and significantly strange. It's a combination you really don't want to be in the South. It's not tolerated. Dumb-and-strange is fine. Smart-and-conservative is admired. Smart-and-strange gets you locked up in the loony bin. Just like my poor old grandma.

I'd have to admit that I'd always been a little ner-

vous about the same thing happening to me sometime. In plenty of nightmares I'd seen Cousin Sylvia,
wide-eyed and unbelieving, standing in the hall at the
hospital, clutching a little rag doll that she used to
talk to in her special language, surrounded by older
people who were babbling in tongues—tongues that
had no diction nor grammar. She was waving good-
bye to me, and I was very ashamed that I didn't wave
back. I was afraid, somehow, that if I waved, they'd
all know I was *like* her—and they'd keep *me* there
too. I hadn't really thought all that much about my
childhood in a very long time. Just as well.

I did my best to match her casual delivery. "So,
where've you been keeping yourself?"

She smiled. "Here and there."

"I'll bet. Do you have any idea where you are
now?" Just checking.

"I'm saying good-bye to the angel. I had to. The
Turners brought me here a few times to talk to the
angel, so I had to tell her good-bye."

"Ah. And?"

"I did. My work is done here. I'm going back to
the sea."

"Yeah, Sylvia . . . or Lydia. Um, that's what I'd
like to talk to you about."

She sighed. "It really is good to see you. You
never can tell, you know."

"I know." But I had no idea what she was talking
about. I was doing what they call *humoring* her. "So.
What've you been doing lately?"

"Oh, this and that, Flap. This and that."

I could see that she had only gotten stranger as

the years had passed—and that was saying something. I was contemplating the problem when Dally came up behind me.

"So it really is her."

I shot her a look that could have knocked over a steamship. "I presume *this* is your little secret?"

"I wasn't *sure* it was your cousin. I only met her once or twice—and I was about six, so I didn't want to say when I wasn't completely sure."

"But you suspected."

"Oh, yeah."

"From the beginning."

"Uh-huh."

"How? What made you suspect?"

She looked down. "I just had a feeling. Sally too. I remembered things . . ."

"And you didn't share. Imagine how that makes me feel."

"Let's not get into this now, Flap."

"Oh, let's. I'm just about as mad at you as I'm ever going to get."

"About *this*?"

I burned her with a look. "Why couldn't you just tell me I might be looking for my own crazy cousin?"

She avoided eye contact. "I know how you feel about your family."

Dalliance Oglethorpe was talking about my aforementioned fear of being crazy myself. When you have a couple of really nutty relatives, you start to worry about your own stability. When you're partly raised by a woman who gets signals from the radio, you have to wonder if any rubbed off. You have a cousin who was shuttled off to a mental hospital when she's seven, you have to think twice about anything out of the ordinary about yourself. And I think just about everybody would agree I was *plenty* out of the ordinary.

So all I could do was nod.

Dally didn't get me in the eye. "Look, I don't want to go over, right now, how much I saw this thing with Lenny get to you. I watched you night after night over in the club, sloshin' down that snooty French grape and figurin' again how you could have done it better, how you messed up, how it all went wrong."

"I don't like to be wrong."

"Yeah, that's my point."

"I don't like loose ends."

"Yeah, I know. You're the neatest straight guy I know."

I was still impatient with her. "So?"

"So I know how reminding you of some of your kin just puts the depression thing into a tailspin sometimes."

"So that's why you didn't let me in on this little secret?"

"I just didn't see the point in even bringing it up if there wasn't anything to it. I didn't think you'd be clear."

"Clear, Dally? *Clear?*"

"I didn't know if you'd be thinkin' right."

Lydia interrupted. She was Lydia now—not Sylvia anymore. I could see that. Okay by me. You can be anybody you want to be, in my book.

She smiled at me. "She's right, Flap. If anybody

ought to know how badly a person's affected by not thinking right, I think you ought to agree it'd be me . . . pretty much?"

I sucked in a deep breath. "Yeah. I guess I'd have to say you know more than your share about that."

The boys couldn't stay away. Maytag slipped up and put his hand on Lydia's shoulder. He was very soft and very sweet. "Hey, darlin'. Glad you remembered to come back here like we told you to—if you was ever lost in Savannah."

You could actually see her face brighten when he touched her, the way some kids respond when they get a clinch from mom. "Hey, Maytag." She peered into the darkness. "Peachy? You out there?"

He appeared. "Sugar-bee. We come to get you home."

She smiled at that too. Okay, so they *were* family, of a sort. You could tell.

Dally let them be. "See?"

I wouldn't have it. "I'm not talking to you, maybe ever again. And this isn't coincidence." I looked all around me in the black night air, and hot as it was, I had a chill. My paranoid genes were acting up—but that's what you get when you're nuts.

Maytag interrupted what could have been a mighty incident between me and my former best friend. "Hey. Mr. Tucker? Thanks for helpin' us find Lydia."

I looked at him. He had the face of an angel himself. Looking at him at that moment, I couldn't believe *anybody* could ever have thought him capable of murder.

And speaking of which, I had to ask, partly to

calm myself down: "So, Lydia, who killed Lowe Acree . . . in *your* opinion? I'm collecting answers."

She looked back at the angel. "Oh, I did. He really deserved it."

I blinked. "He deserved it?"

"Oh, my, yes." She closed her eyes.

I looked at Dally, still a little out of sorts with her. "Well, I'm going to have to sit down to hear this one."

So we marched our little party back to the benches where Dally and I had contemplated French Symbolists and thieves. We all sat down. It was a late-night historical discussion group, or a ghost hunters' club in a boneyard.

I began. "Okay, then, Lydia: Spill. What's the story?"

She didn't know quite how to start. "Well . . ."

Maytag finally got it. "Wait a minute." He looked at me. "I just figured out: You know Lydia some kinda way."

I looked at the ground. "She's my cousin. My grandmother's brother was her grandfather."

That just confused him. "Grandmother's . . . grandfather . . ."

I shifted. "I knew her when we were kids. Haven't seen her in a really long while. Last I saw of her, they'd carted her away to Milledgeville."

Milledgeville State Mental Hospital—in the old days you'd make fun of other kids by saying, "Are you from Milledgeville or something?" Like everybody in the town was off. Wouldn't have wanted to be on their city council back then.

She nodded. "Yeah. I was in and out of that place for years."

I took a little breath. "Really?"

"Well, when I was in there first time, you know, Momma and Daddy died."

I nodded. "Now that you mention it, I think there was talk around our house about it." It was coming back to me. They'd killed themselves in a suicide pact. They'd thought the end of the world was just around the corner. That's why they'd taken Sylvia/Lydia, their only daughter, to the mental hospital. She'd refused to join them. Even at her young age she'd tried to reason with them. Their response had been to lock her up. This may explain to all and sundry the further complications of the concept "It runs in the family." I could only imagine what it would do to me if I'd been locked up when I was that young—and then my folks had iced themselves on top of it. I looked over at Dalliance, and all of a sudden I wasn't completely mad anymore. I was just thankful I'd had a pal like her since I was a kid. Plenty better than having to face it all alone, like Lydia'd had to.

Lydia went on. "I was adopted by the Habershams. They couldn't have children. When I got out of Milledgeville, I went to an orphanage in Hapeville. They got me there. They had all my names legally changed. It was their idea of giving me a fresh start."

Dally was curious about that one. "Fresh start?"

"The Habershams knew my family history, but they didn't really think I was insane. The only real reason *they* ever used to send me off to the hospital every once in a while, when I got older, was that I was what they called a wild child. If I did something they thought was strange, they'd pack me off again. Most of the time it was something really small. Like once I wanted to get a tattoo of a mermaid on my forearm. It was my Popeye phase. That made them really nervous.'"

I nodded. "I met them. I can imagine."

Dally jumped in. "Yeah. Okay. Whatever. I guess what I'm really more interested in is why you'd marry Lowe Acree in the first place. He was just, like, the town bully or something—him and his cousin, Tommy. What was the attraction?"

"He said he loved me."

Dally gave her a look. "Uh-huh."

She smiled. "My head'd been messed with so much at that point, I would have believed it if he'd told me I was Santa Claus. I just would have started handing out presents."

My turn. "Uh-huh. There's got to be more. Maybe there's a story that goes with it. Ms. Oglethorpe loves a good story."

28

A Marriage Proposal

Lydia obliged. She told us how she'd been minding her own business, as much as she could, when something wicked came her way—in the form of a rich, handsome businessman.

"Miss? Excuse me, ma'am?"

She dropped her rigging, slung herself over the hold, and looked at the guy on the dock. "Uh-huh."

"Are you Lydia Habersham?"

"Yup."

"June over at the DeSoto told me about you. I'd like very much to catch me a big old fish. She says you're the best."

"She's a friend."

"My name is Lowe? Lowe Acree? I got a bank over in Tifton, and I got a few weeks off, here. I was hoping to start now and go all weekend, at least."

"It's seven hundred and fifty dollars a day."

"Whoa. Everybody else is five hundred, tops."

"Then go with everybody else."

"How come you're so much more?"

"Keeps out the pikers."

Lowe Acree smiled. "Uh-huh. Well, then. I'm no piker. When do we leave."

"Shove your stuff up on deck. I'll cast off."

Her hair was nearly white from being in the sun all the time, but her skin was still pale. She took Lowe's elbow as he came on board. "I got some number-two-hundred sunblock, or some such. I think it even keeps out X rays. I use it and I never even tan. I suggest you put some on. The sun's brutal out there."

He waved her off. "Aw, I could use a little sun on me."

She shrugged. "Suit yourself."

They were underway in five minutes. Lydia was very good. That day Lowe caught a marlin, a shark, and about half a dozen smaller fish. He decided to keep them all.

When the sun was setting, and Lowe was putting some Intensive Care lotion on his sunburn, they headed west, toward the coast.

"Well, Lydia—this has indeed been a day worth the money."

"Yup."

"Could I interest you in a little beverage over at June's at the DeSoto? Maybe a bite of dinner? My treat."

"I don't think so."

"Come on. No harm. I do believe you are the

most beautiful woman I ever saw in my life. What color hair is that?"

"Usually what they call auburn, but the sun's bleached it out. I don't know what they'd call it now."

"They'd call it remarkable."

"Uh-huh."

"You're not buying any of this, I see."

"Nope."

"You don't intend to go out with me."

She throttled the engine. They were coming into dock. "Nope."

"No matter what."

"That's right."

"Not even for somebody rich enough to set you free."

She laughed. "Free from what?"

He looked out to sea. "Well, how about from your parents? Parents that bounce you off to some mental hospital every time you get a slightly unusual notion in your head."

Lydia made a face. "That damn June. She has to tell everybody everything about me."

He was serious. "Look. I'm somebody who knows what it's like to be a wild child in a dead garden."

She just stared. "Nice turn of the phrase."

"You know what I'm talking about. I'm a wild boy in my hometown. The only difference is, I happen to *run* a lot of it."

Lowe Acree went to the wheel. Lydia had stopped piloting her little boat, and Lowe took charge. He guided the vessel safely homeward. While he did, he spoke very softly to her. "I'd like to have a little talk with your parents. I'd like to ask them for your hand."

She didn't bother looking at him. She didn't know what to say. "They're not really my parents, you know."

He smiled. She didn't see it. He spoke even softer. "I know."

"I'm adopted." She was watching the sun set out over the water.

The boat knocked the side of the dock; Lowe secured it. "Feel like scallops? They got a great coquilles Saint Jacques over at The Hut."

"I know."

He smiled. "I guess if you told anybody about this . . . I mean, imagine how insane all this would sound. You meet a guy one day and he spends a few hours with you and he knows for good and all that he wants to marry you. I mean it—I imagine how really out-of-touch this must sound."

She was slowly regaining her composure. She had a method. It was simple. Whenever the events of her life threatened to capsize the still, small boat of her mind, she imagined calm waves on the shore of a golden beach and said the word *waves* over and over to herself as she breathed out. Events in life were just waves on the sand. No more. No less. Just waves. No value, no meaning, no import. No other thoughts or images were allowed to permeate this single-mindedness of the image; the repeated word. And in a while, she was calm.

She finally looked at Lowe. "As it happens, imagining how insane all this would sound is one of the few things I'm really good at."

"Plus, knowing where the marlins are."

She actually smiled. "That too."

"So. Scallops?"

She smiled. "What could happen—it's just a few scallops."

Lowe went to the refrigerated hold and checked his fish. "This is going to be some good eating. You can make arrangements to have it cut up and frozen and sent to my home?"

Lydia nodded.

Lowe helped her off the boat, and as they walked toward The Hut, he took her hand. "I'll treat you so well. I'll never do anything you don't want me to do. Everything will be all right. You'll always be the perfect girl for me, and I'll always love you. You'll never want for anything, and as far as this part of the world is concerned, you'll be kind of like royalty, Southern aristocracy. It'll be just like a dream."

And so they were married. There was a big wedding. All of Savannah's aristocracy was there—along with a few guests from Beautiful. Then the blushing bride went, like Ruth, into another land: Tifton. Where her husband went, she would go. His people would be her people. His home would be her home. She became Mrs. Lydia Habersham Acree—and not one of those three names was actually her own. It was, in fact, very much like a dream. But what Lowe Acree had in mind was a different kind of dream altogether.

39

The Belly of the Beast

What Lowe Acree had in mind was a nightmare.
Lowe had forgotten to mention that he had a temper,
and that this temper was often enhanced by the use
of a drug he concocted by means of his connection
with a very lucrative chemical franchise. It was a
combination of heroin, cocaine, and a remedy for
seasickness. He injected himself with this drug, and
his talent for prodigious violence became Promethean.
On many occasions it occurred to him to give Lydia
some of the same drug, but his greed always pre-
vented it. He wanted it all for himself. Besides, she
didn't need it. She was so frightened when he was in
these moods that she'd do anything he said.

She got lost in a kind of trance after a while.
None of it was real to her, the whole marriage idea.
It all started seeming . . . well, like a dream. As
promised.

"Every time he'd take the drug, he'd get worse.
First it was just yelling and hitting. Then it was little

games he'd play—stalking and . . . I don't know."
She shrugged. "I just came to accept it as a normal
part of my life, like any other incident: no value, no
import. Just another wave. I didn't have any other
way of dealing with it. I couldn't see a way out.
Maybe that sounds strange—but you don't know
how a thing like that is from the *inside* unless you've
been there yourself."

Maytag made as to get up and go to her, but
Dally put her hand on his arm. Lydia was deep in
some dark place now—you don't wake up a sleep-
walker, they say.

"Then there was a moment that Lowe's violence
got beyond his ability to control it. It was a dilly. He
wanted to meet some men out beyond the legal limit
of the country, out on the high seas. These men had a
huge supply of heroin and a bigger supply of cocaine, and they were willing to sell it to Lowe for lots
of money."

Dally shifted. She knew something rough was
coming. I don't know how, but I could tell she was
about to get up and go away.

"The day began like any other in the previous
weeks. I ended up piloting the boat out to sea and he
got wasted, started threatening to toss me over-
board. I started yelling back at him, and he whacked
me good in the head maybe a couple dozen times. I
went down."

All this was with no hint of strangeness or disgust. It was all just a part of the play. She was just an
actor, strutting and fretting her hour away.

"I couldn't breathe, I think he might have broken my nose. I must have passed out. Lowe was

too far gone to know that I'd lapsed into deep unconsciousness."

She closed her eyes.

Maytag got up. "Stop."

Peachy took him by the arm, nudged him away. Maytag didn't resist. I think he might have been crying.

Lydia just went on. "I think surely Lowe, at the time, must have been farther away from normalcy than he'd ever been. He was in the middle of his deal with these drug men. I'm sure he said it didn't matter about me. He said to just leave me. They'd come back later. They'd revive me. I'm guessing the men gave him a ride back to shore to where he'd stashed the money. They just left the drugs on board with me. Everything would be fine. Why worry? Everything was taken care of. Nothing to worry about."

I had to stop her. She was about to lose it. "Hey, Lydia . . ."

But it only served to prompt her farther into the story. "As they were leaving, I vaguely remember the youngest man, a Cuban boy really . . . he helped me to the cot down in the hold. I was barely breathing."

Dally was up now, wandering a little way off, like it was a botany lecture in which she had little interest, but I could tell she was still listening.

"I have no idea how long I slept. When I woke up, everyone was gone. I roused myself, not really sure of anything that had gone on."

I suddenly remembered something. "Hey. On your boat. There's a copy of *Lamb's Tales from Shakespeare*. That yours?"

She smiled and nodded, a little released from the

awful spell of the memory of that day. "You remember that book?"

I smiled back. "Sorta." I looked over at Dally. "Charles and Mary Lamb, they tell the stories from Shakespeare's plays to little kids—like me and Lydia, at the time."

Dally was anxious to get the story over with. "The point is?"

I shrugged. "It was something of a clue. Probably one of the things that made Sylvia/Lydia show up in my dream deal."

Dally was still too impatient. She looked at Lydia. "So, you stayed out at sea?"

She nodded. "Found the drugs on my boat and tossed them over the side. Cleaned up the boat. Threw all my clothes away—just like Flap's grandma. I moved the boat around in the sea, over by some of the smaller islands, where they wouldn't find me. Swam for hours every day in the salty water, washing it all away. Over and over I just kept saying *waves*. The sky was blue, the sea was calm, the days were numberless. The mind was clearing. Got back in the boat. Headed home."

Dally was confused. "You had no clothes?"

"Nothing I'd ever worn in my relationship with Lowe—I made sure of that. I found one of my old swimming suits in a cedar chest under the guest bed."

"How long did it take you to get back?"

She shrugged. "I don't know. But there was a big fuss when I got there. They said I'd been gone nearly three weeks."

I nodded. "Yeah. I saw the newspaper article at June's."

"Lowe was waiting for me at home—I mean my parent's home. They'd all agreed that the situation—my being gone so long—was too strange to let me wander around unsecured from then on. The parents didn't even want to listen to my version of the story. I could go back to the mental hospital, or I could stay married. That was that." She looked at one of the grave markers. "I still thought—even after all that—it wasn't a bad way to get out from under the folks at home. I couldn't bear to be with them. I think they call it being between the devil and the deep blue sea."

Maytag and Peachy were milling around a little ways off. They didn't care to hear any more. Dally had nodded her head through most of the tale, her eyes nearly closed. I was feeling a little like I had the flu, my own self.

Lydia was droning on. "I have absolutely no idea why Lowe thought he'd want to marry me. Whacking me for no reason, yelling at me in church. We went to church, can you believe it? When his boss, the president of the bank, got married to some secretary half his age? I made the mistake of crying at the wedding. It just made me so sad to see that girl marrying a man old enough to be her father just so she could have money. Lowe beat me up right there in the church. Most of the people just pretended not to see it, can you imagine? That was just before Lowe died." She fixed a gaze on me. "Why do people want money so much, Flap?"

"I don't know."

"Don't you?"

"Nope. I'm motivated by other things."

"Like . . . what?"

"Well, right at the moment I wouldn't mind finding Lowe Acree alive and killing him all over again. Thinking I'd bury him up to his neck in calamari, and use his melon for batting practice."

"Nice image."

"Thanks. And these things I would do for the love of it. Money would not be my object."

"So you can't tell me why people are like Lowe."

"Nope. I can't tell you because I just don't know."

"Well, then."

I wanted to let her off the hook, get some rest, but I still needed some other information.

"Sugar? Where . . . where do you reckon you've been all this time? I mean, while the cops and the Turner twins and June and half the police force of Savannah—not to mention yours very truly—have been searching everywhere for you?"

"I've been with a kid named Ronnie Tibadeau."

Just shove a lightning bolt up the back of my neck, why don't you.

"Ronnie Tibadeau?"

"Yeah, he's a grungy little runner for Lowe and Tommy. I'm pretty sure he ran up to Atlanta now and again with supplies for the drug dealers there. Anyway, he and Tommy Acree found me at the house out on the island. . . ."

"Okay, I'll bite. Which island?"

"Cumberland?"

"Pretty, post—Frank Lloyd Wright job with an upstairs?"

"Yes. How do you—?"

"—I've been there."

Nothing surprised her that night. "Okay. Anyway, they found me there. Wasn't that hard, really. It's where I *always* go to get away from trouble in these parts."

They must have collected her just before the Turner boys got there. Timing's everything, even in weirdness. "So where did they take you?"

"I don't know. Someplace around here."

"When?"

"Flap, honest, I don't know. Time is a little . . . skewed just now."

"So how'd you get here tonight?"

"Tommy came by and let me go. Then he and Ronnie had a fight." She closed her eyes. "Or maybe they had a fight and let me go—maybe that was it."

I wasn't going to let her go over the edge just now. I had to keep her on the beam. "Just how much of this do you think Tommy Acree is into?"

"He's a policeman. He's Lowe's cousin."

"Yeah, him."

"Gee, I don't know. He knew a lot about it. He and Lowe were going into business together. They wanted to buy the Turner land and set up a manufacturing plant for Lowe's drug."

"Yeah—they call it Homicide."

"What?"

"That's what they call it, the drug you say he was taking."

"Whatever. He was going to use that land as a

place to make it. It's really private. Tommy knew about all that. They were going to make a fortune."

I wanted to be sure. "Tommy knew."

"Tommy *invested*."

I nodded. "How come the boys wouldn't sell the land?"

"They thought Lowe was going to use it for a chemical dump. That's what he told everybody."

Maytag's voice came out of the darkness behind me. "Maybe this is important, maybe it ain't. But it just come to me *one* reason why Lowe could have been so interested in Lydia. See, me an' Peach? We arranged, a good while back, with our family lawyer, that if anything ever happened to us, that particular land would go over to Lydia."

The silence was only a backdrop for crickets and tree frogs.

Lydia and Dally and I were giving them one very strenuous look.

Dally said it before anyone else did. "Yeah, that might explain why Lowe was sweet on you, honey. He always figured he could get the boys declared incompetent—or maybe he even had the idea that they'd get dead somehow—and then the land would be yours. And since you're nutty in the fruit basket . . . no offense . . ."

She smiled. ". . . none taken . . ."

Dally finished. ". . . and he was your husband, the land would be his."

I popped another look at the boys. "Now, why would you give the land over to Lydia?"

They looked at me like I couldn't even speak English.

Maytag shook his head. "We don't have that much money to speak of, but we do have land. It's all we got, to give to our family."

Peachy agreed. "We love her, Flap. She's family."

I was about to launch into a very long tirade about the nature of family, when there was another voice in the darkness—and right on cue, if you ask me.

40

Summer Freeze

"Everybody just stand real still." Tommy Acree stepped into the dim light that bounced off the gravestones from the streetlamps not so far away. His gun was poised and his hand was steady. "Boy"—he actually laughed out loud—"you are all so *very* under arrest." You could tell he wanted to shoot *something* real bad.

Maytag spoke like a little kid. "Hey, Tommy." Remember how the little girl says "Hey, Boo" to Robert Duvall in *To Kill a Mockingbird*? That voice.

Tommy's eyes were dancing. "Lord, I done hit the jackpot." He was looking at the five of us like we were buried treasure. "Now I wished I hadn't sent Taylor and everybody else on home. I just had a hunch"—more laughing—"but I didn't expect this. I surely would have brought my fellow officers of the law along with me."

I kept my hands very calm, and right where he

could see them. "Okay, *Tom,* here's the deal: Put the gun down and get away from me."

He wasn't even the least bit irritated. "Why would I want to do that?"

"Because if you don't, all kinds of hell is going to befall all over you."

"Sorry?"

I took a little step toward him. "First, I know about the drugs. I know Lowe was a bad man—maybe you are too. Second, I know why you wanted the Turner land. And third, I believe I know how Lowe died. It has almost *nothing* to do with anybody you're looking at. Not to mention that between me and Maytag and Peachy, you're going down like a broken elevator."

He wasn't moved. "I don't care what you know. I got you good. There's a big old dead body over there under your car, bud. I conked him on the head, wired your car, ran over him, and then handcuffed the body to the chassis. You're in absolutely the most trouble you've ever been in. Maybe I'll just shoot you now for resisting arrest and have done with it."

I sucked in a breath. I couldn't deal with Ronnie Tibadeau just then. I had to let Tommy know who was boss. "I already told you: I don't care about that. And I'm standing pretty close. I doubt you'd kill me before I got a hold of you. Then you'd be in all kinds of hurt."

Peachy strolled up to me calmly. "He ain't gonna shoot you, Mr. Tucker."

Maytag agreed. "He's comprised of nearly one hundred percent chicken manure. He don't got the guts to clean fish."

Peachy explained it to me. "Him and Lowe? They used to beat up on people all the time in high school."

Maytag agreed. "They were what you'd call delinquent."

I remembered. "The Peaker Brother-morticians had a few things to say along those lines."

Peachy wasn't finished. "But they'd never do it unless there was only one to beat up on—and *both* of them Acrees."

Maytag looked at Tommy. "There's only one of you now, bud—and a whole mess-buncha *us*."

Tommy waved the gun a little wildly. "You're forgetting about this."

Peachy laughed. "What? That little old thing? I hurt myself worse shavin' than you could wi' that." And he launched himself toward the policeman.

Tommy panicked. You could see it in his eyes. I don't think he even meant to, but he started spraying bullets. Peachy was hit right away—leg, I think. I caught something a second later, just where I part my hair. But we got him. In less than ten seconds Tommy Acree was flat on the ground with five hundred pounds of mad redneck all over him, and me looking down at the mess. Peachy was dabbing at his leg, but it didn't seem to bother him much.

I had the gun in my hand. Then I started feeling my head. "Damn. I think you shot me. Tommy, can you see this? Am I shot here?"

But he was in no condition to answer. Dally was right there; got a good peep at my noggin; pronounced me alive. All through the ruckus Lydia just stood there smiling, like it was all a dream.

Peachy looked up at Dally. "What're we gonna do with 'im?"

She sighed. "Let's take him back to the nightclub. Maybe he'll cool off and we can get somethin' settled, here, about all this brouhaha." She eyeballed me. "Including your mechanic friend, Ronnie."

The boys had to bop Tommy a couple before he'd calm down, but they got him to his feet, and we were off.

Once again, what a sight we must have been: Dally in the lead; Tommy in between the football stars; me and Lydia, arm in arm, bringing up the tail of the grand parade.

Peachy called out in a stage whisper. "Hey, Ms. Oglethorpe. What'd you say you was callin' your new nightclub place?"

"Too Easy."

"Oh. Good name."

Without turning, she aimed her voice at me. I could well imagine the look on her face. "It's not a name, it's a way of life."

I wasn't absolutely sure, but I thought just maybe, in that moment the sun might be coming up over the old churchyard. The long night was nearly over.

41

The Big Dream

We settled into the backroom of Dally's new club. We didn't know what else to do, so we tied Tommy up to a chair like you see in the movies. Now, ordinarily a guy like me will avoid tying up an officer of the law like it was the swine flu. But under the circumstances—we had in fact resisted arrest, roughed the guy up, *and* accused him of all manner of heinous crimes and whatnot—a little chair-tying seemed the next logical step.

There in the first light of day I was the last one standing at the future Too Easy. Lydia was lying down on a drop cloth, trying to sleep. The boys were making coffee and making a lot of noise horsing around with something in the other room. Dally was in what was left of an armchair. It was pretty beat-up. I guess it must have been left by the previous managers of the establishment.

I tried to speak to Detective Acree with as much deference as I could muster. "Now, Tommy, if you'll let me, I think I can tell you how your cousin Lowe died."

He spit. "I know how he died. Those retards in the other room—who, incidentally, don't seem to be able to figure out the coffeemaker, let alone any kind of alibi—beat my cousin's head into his own desk."

"Not quite. They choked him, but they didn't kill him."

"What?"

"They got him in a choke hold so he'd quit whacking his wife."

He squinted. I think he might have even twitched. "She wasn't even there."

Sleepily, from the drop cloth: "Yes, I was. I was hiding in the bathroom."

I continued. "Apparently Lowe had a private bath in his office."

Tommy was not amused. "I know what he had in his office."

"I don't think you do." I raised my voice. "Maytag, you boys about finished in there?"

Peachy's head popped around the corner, grinning. "They got a hula hoop in here."

"Cool, but could you all come on in?"

From the other room I could hear Maytag: "Awww."

But they came. Lydia sat up. Dally had a look of mirth I hadn't seen in a while from her. Used to be a regular look. I was happy to see it back.

As the boys were filing in, I had to ask her about it. "What's so funny?"

She shook her head. "Just good to see you in your element."

I looked around. "Naw. This place hasn't been my element for quite a while."

"Not what I meant."

I had to smile back then. "I know. And by the way? I was just thinking the same kind of thing about you."

She actually blushed. I have no idea why.

But we didn't pursue it. The stage was set. I guess I *was* in my element, at that. It was the time of the day to let all shadows brush away. I was on.

"Stop me when I go wrong, anybody. But, Lydia? The day Lowe died, he called you up on the phone and told you to come over to the bank."

Tommy was impatient with me. "How in this world would you know a thing like that?"

Lydia yawned. "He's right."

I gave Tommy the eye. "Given the tenor of their relationship as I now understand it, I can't really see her going over to his workplace of her own volition." I went on to Lydia. "He called you to bring him a shot, I'm guessing. He said something like he had a meeting with the Turner twins and he wanted to be *prepared* for it, so you were to bring him one of his syringes."

She was a little more alert, riveted, no doubt, by my acute awareness of the events of her life.

"Right. How would you know that?"

I blinked. "I'm good at guessing. You gave him the fatal shot. Why else would you think you'd killed the guy? Unless you really *did* whisper a magic word in his ear that made his brain explode. I'm not entirely ruling that out as a possibility, knowing you as I do."

She just nodded, thinking.

"So—when you got there, you tried to talk him out of it."

She couldn't take it anymore. "This is amazing. It's like you were there."

Dally answered. "He's got a trick."

I finished. "Plus, it's the only thing that makes any sense out of the events."

Tommy was unconvinced. He spat out a German-sounding word that has something to do with carnal knowledge in the English penal system.

I was undaunted. "Be that as it may, Tom, Lydia was only trying to save your cousin from himself. Plus, as we've discussed among ourselves, Lowe would apparently get even meaner than he normally was after he'd taken that shot—so she was trying to do herself a favor too."

Lydia nodded silently.

I went on. "But Lowe wouldn't hear of it. He insisted on his shot. Lydia gave it to him. And he was *already* mad because he'd had to argue with Lydia to get it. I'm saying he was *plenty* steamed when the boys showed up, a little early." I looked at Lydia. "How'm I doing? Still on the beam?"

Lydia confirmed.

"He told you to hide . . . like, in the bathroom so he could dispatch the twins, get their land, make the deal. Whatever. You hid. Lowe yelled. The boys resisted. You popped out from the bathroom, trying to leave—or maybe trying to help the boys. Lowe wouldn't let you. The boys took exception. They got Lowe into a choke hold. He started to pass out."

She was sitting up now, completely awake.

I nodded at her; she nodded back. I looked back at Tommy. "She could see there was something wrong with him. His face bugged out or something. My guess at this point is that he'd made the dose too strong. All the activity with the boys sped everything up and he went into shock. Maybe it was in combination with the exertion or the lack of breath, whatever. The drug zapped him in his brain pan and fell down on his whatchamacallit and he was dead."

Lydia couldn't seem to quit nodding.

Tommy's eyes were on her now, like a searchlight, like a lighthouse beacon. She seemed about to tumble over the edge again.

She started to get to her feet, but she couldn't. "That's right. I gave him his shot. He said that's what he wanted. He was asking for it. So I gave it to him. I killed my husband. That's what this story means: I killed him."

Maytag shook his head. "Nuh-uh, darlin'. It was me that was chokin' him to death."

Peachy wouldn't hear of it. "In point of fact it was me that let him slip down in his seat so he banged his head. That's what did it. Absolutely my fault." He looked at Tommy. "I apologize." Like he'd spilled Lowe's coffee on his desk.

She was still nodding, like one of those dumb dogs some people have in the back window of their cars. "I gave him the shot. I killed him."

Tommy was still glued to Lydia, and his face was different than I'd yet seen it: contorted, strange, devoid of all the self-assurance and bravado I'd noted there in our earlier encounter. His voice was very soft, and kinder than I would have imagined it could be. "Lydia? Honey? It's not your fault. It's not you at all."

"I gave him the shot. I did. I'm the one."

"Maybe you did, but he was asking for it."

She was right on the brink. "Doesn't matter. I killed a man."

"No, you didn't."

She closed her eyes. "I gave him the shot that killed him."

I thought Tommy was going to cry or explode or roll on the floor like at a church meeting. "But you're not the one that . . . you didn't make up the . . . you didn't make it to where it was too strong to take . . ." But he couldn't finish his thought. He let go his gaze. He was trying hard to see something in one of the cracks in the floor. He wanted to die. It might as well have been written on a sign around his neck.

I think I got it before anybody else. Maybe it was something somebody at the family reunion at the Kingdom Baptist had mentioned before about their suspicions about Tommy Acree. Maybe it was something in his eyes when he looked at Lydia. "That's right, Lydia. You didn't make up the shot and put too much juice in it." I eyed Lowe's cousin for all he was worth. "Tommy did that. Didn't you, Tommy?"

He was still staring at the floor. His voice was like an electric shaving razor, tinny and growling: "I don't know whether I thought it would kill him . . . or not. I just don't know." He looked at me. Maybe he was asking my opinion. "What could I do? He was killing her. Everybody could see that. He beat her in front of everybody in church one day. Can you imagine that? In *church*. He was using her like she

was a rag doll, like she was a . . . something not real.
He didn't love her." Suddenly he really wanted to
know my answer. "How could he do it? How could
he do those awful things?"

I helped. "To the woman *you* loved."

No thunder, no lightning, no special effects at all.
He just nodded, looking down at the floor again.

Lydia blinked hard; talked slow. "What?"

Maytag looked at him, no disgust, no sympathy,
just fact: "Well, Mr. Acree . . . if *that's* true, you seem
to be more messed up of a person than just about
anybody around, in my opinion."

Peachy thought so too. "Now that Lowe's dead."

Dally seemed to find it all strangely amusing in
the grand scheme of things. She let a moment of silence pass before she had her say. "So now *everybody* wants to take credit for killing Lowe Acree."

Tommy looked at her. "I got into his house . . .
just that morning. That very morning. It was after he
left for work and when Lydia went to the store. I saw
her go. I knew he would want a taste when he dealt
with the twins. He always said it gave him the killer
instinct in the business deals." He looked at Peachy.
"Not that he'd need it with those two. Still, I knew
he'd take him some." He looked to me for support,
it seemed. "See, I thought he'd come home for it. I
didn't have any idea he'd be crazy enough to do it at
work. I just didn't figure on anybody else getting involved. He'd just shoot up, conk out, that'd be it.
Junkie overdose. If he was just really sick or knocked
out, I'd find him, take him to the hospital, he'd be
exposed—maybe even get help. I'd like to believe I
had that in my head. But if he died, I'd be stunned.

The town'd gossip about it for months. But by and by something else would happen that would take their minds off it and they'd be on to something else. That'd be that. I'd console the widow—respectfully. I'd wait six months more. We'd date. Everything would be fine—eventually." He twisted around so he could face Lydia full on. "I'd have treated you so good. You just don't know. You would have been like a queen."

She smiled. "That's what Lowe said." But there was no meanness in her voice.

I was more on the mean side. "That's why you didn't allow an autopsy?"

He was back to me. "I just couldn't be sure. With him dead it was just as well if nothing else came up. I mean . . . I was connected to it too. But it was perfect the way it was, see. I could blame the twins for the murder, get their land anyway, be a hero for finding my cousin's killers—same ending as before: happily ever after. I just never figured on . . . I never thought she'd be there." He looked at her like he was on his deathbed looking at the angels. "If I'd known you were there . . ."

Dally sat back. "The girl of your dreams."

He shot a glance back to Lydia. "Look at her. "She's the girl of everybody's dreams."

Well, she'd certainly been such stuff as dreams were made on. You had to give her that. Still, I was a little skeptical. "So, Tommy? Why this sudden confession? I mean, why all this talk now? Why tell us everything?"

"She's been through enough. I never figured on

your finding her. I never figured on your being capable of that. You don't seem like you could find your way to your own shoes, to me, you don't have the gumption—but I guess you've got your ways." Back to the floor again, like the magic words were written there, the ones that could make Lydia well. "I didn't think it all through, I guess." Once again, to yours truly. "I didn't plan on your being even remotely motivated enough to pursue all this. You seem on the lazy side."

I wasn't offended. "Yeah, but I'm lucky."

Dally wouldn't hear of it, though. She's really a swell friend to have, after everything's said and done. "Luck's got nothin' to do with it. He's got a trick." She popped me a look that could light up a city block. "His cosmology is the entire human spirit."

I smiled big. "Boy, you got a memory on you could choke a horse."

She shook her head. "I remember what I want to."

The boys didn't understand, but they nodded like they did.

Dally nudged the moment toward a more immediate concern. "Say, Tom—by the way? What do you think Ronnie's doing out there under Flap's car?"

He wouldn't look us in the eye now. That spot on the floor must have been absolutely fascinating. "Ronnie did us favors."

I wanted him to tell the story, even though I felt I now knew how it went, so I chimed in. "So I'm told. Did they include drug-running to Atlanta? I've got a friend in the business is why I'm asking."

"Sometimes."

I nodded. "Go on."

"So I got him to bug your car. Then I got him to come along with me to help clean up this mess down here, and I needed somebody to watch Lydia while I took care of the boys; you—whatever else came up." Softer. "I just wanted to make sure she was all right."

Dally wouldn't let up. "So?"

"So . . . I was pretty sure she'd be out at that house on Cumberland. It's where she usually went when she ran away from Lowe, or when she was confused. She was there, just sitting on the porch. When I told her Lowe was dead, she just shrugged."

I was impatient. "Skip on down."

He shifted; looked at me. "Ronnie was a boy, a little boy. He wasn't bad, but he had a troubled personality. He was really little more than a stupid petty criminal. I should never have left him with Lydia."

Lydia spoke up. "It was nothing."

He was suddenly very hot. "The *hell* it was."

Dally intruded once more. "Get on with the story."

He stabbed a look her way, but went on then. "He was touching her when I came back from finding Mr. Tucker at the same house on Cumberland. He was touching her hair."

Lydia started to stand. "It was nothing, Tommy. He was just petting my head." She looked at me. "We were at a little bed-and-breakfast just around the corner from the graveyard."

I had to ask. "So, Tom—why didn't you just take her over to her parents' house?"

He shook his head violently. "Those drunks. They wouldn't know how to handle sitting *down,* not even

262 Phillip DePoy

with a set of instructions and a diagram. She didn't need zookeepers." He tried to look at her, but he couldn't—like she was too bright, like he was looking into the sun. "She needed me."

I nodded. "And when you got there, to the bed-and-breakfast, Ronnie was messing with her."

"I whipped his ass around so fast his brains nearly came out. I shook him like a big old empty gunnysack, but I could see it was upsetting Lydia, so I took him into the bathroom."

Lydia was almost to her feet then. "I could hear them arguing."

He looked at me, not at her. "I popped him a good one on the jaw. He fell back into the sink. Didn't kill him, but it didn't do him any good. He was out."

I knew what was what. "That's when you got the idea: let Lydia go, let her go where she might lead you to the boys."

He didn't even ask how I guessed that. He just nodded. "I came back in, told her she could go."

Lydia was up now, staring at him. "I'd already told Ronnie I wanted to go back to the sea. I told him my work was done here. He said he couldn't let me go. But he was sorry. That's why he was petting my head, because he was sorry."

Tommy was more frazzled. "I didn't know what I was doing. I told her to leave; got Ronnie up; called some of my seedier associates here in Savannah; shoved him into my car. I don't think she had any idea I was right behind her all the way when she was walking over here. I saw her go into the graveyard. I have no idea how long she wandered around in there looking at tombstones while I was taking care of Ronnie."

She was moving to him. "I was going back to the sea—I was trying to say good-bye to the angel but I heard voices so I stayed in the shadows."

He looked at me, almost ignoring her, like he was explaining. "I should never have let her out of my sight but for a minute. I mean, that's how she was talking: that angel crap."

She was very close now. "I just wanted to say good-bye." She cocked her head. "Hey—I left my parasol there."

I nodded. "Yeah, I saw it over there. What were you doing with an umbrella anyway?"

She shook her head. "Parasol. I always have it, to keep out the sun. Last thing I need is to sunburn this lily skin—and I like the little shadow. I'm not sure I want to see everything I see—not that clearly. See what I'm saying?"

Tommy looked like he was trying to move away from her then, trying to ignore her severe strangeness—maybe because it's one of the things he found so attractive about her. But what do I know?

He looked at me instead. "I couldn't believe it when I saw your car out there. Jesus. I nearly had a wreck stopping." He was shaking his head pretty good now. "I really don't know what I was thinking at that point. I was pretty full up." Full up with what, he did not report. "I unloaded Ronnie. It was nothing. I hot-wired your car like it was meant to start that way. I laid Ronnie in the road, and ran your heap over him good, three, four times. He was pretty dead after that. Then I called my guys to come and get you. They were right around the corner. I should have known better than to call a set of junkie brothers."

I smiled. "Only one's a junkie. The other's a storyteller."

Tommy Acree started to ask me all sorts of questions, then stopped in what seemed like mid thought and looked at me like a kid. "What was the matter with me? What was I doing? How'd I let it get to this?"

Lydia was beside him now, like a column of fire, burning that side of his face. She reached out and touched him very softly, it seemed to me. He flinched like it singed him.

She whispered. "It's all a dream, Tommy. And it's not even your dream. Isn't that funny? Don't worry. There's nothing to worry about. It'll all be just fine."

Big silence.

42

The Deal

Peachy wanted to move on. "What now?"

I started. "Well, now . . ." But I had nowhere to go. "I don't know."

And who would have figured, but it was Lydia came up with the first plan. She got to her feet and announced it like she was giving a speech at the Optimist Club.

"Now we go home. The story's over. We have Tommy arrested by the Savannah police—five witnesses to his confession. Maybe we'll call that nice boy that plays the viola. He loves me—talked to me all the time at June's. Then we exhume Lowe's body for proof. Then we destroy all the drugs he's got, and that's that. Then we go back to our families—I maybe go live with the Turners on their farm if it turns out that I'm not entirely a creature from the sea, which it seems possible to me at this point that I might not be, and . . . then . . ." But she was running out of steam then too.

It had been a long dark night for her. It had taken a lot out of her to set up the whole vision of grand retribution. She'd seen the whole wheel of the cosmos in motion. It's a rare vision. I've had it once or twice myself. It's absolutely exhausting. But she was in a better frame of mind than she had been for a while, anybody could see that.

I had to be the one to bust her bubble. "Not quite, sugar. See, no matter what, in that scenario you're the one who actually wielded the murder device. So there'd be a little problem with it: You could still go to jail, or worse."

She understood immediately. "Especially considering I'm loonier than a peanut farm."

"There *is* that."

"So what?"

The room fell silent. Most seemed to be waiting for me to make with the wise pronouncements. I took a shot.

"Tommy? Lowe was your cousin, and I'm sure you have some good memories of him."

He shook his head. He didn't want to play.

I wanted him to. "Come on. One good memory. It'll make you feel better about all this, I guarantee."

He was willing to reminisce if it was like a part of the confession. "We used to go bass fishing when we were kids."

It wasn't enough for me. "And?"

And then he actually smiled. "It was so much fun. He'd cut up in the boat so big that we fell in the lake half the time; didn't care a bit. Part of the fun. Didn't hardly ever catch a thing; didn't care about that either."

"Okay, but he turned out to be a very bad man, wouldn't you agree?"

Tommy took his time, but he nodded after a while. "He got that way."

"So let's put Lowe to rest once and for all. What if our plan goes this way: New evidence—that *you* uncover—indicates that Lowe was—oh, my God— some kind of drug fiend. Maybe you find the drugs in his house or something in his papers or whatever. You request an autopsy. That'll prove he died of a drug overdose, confirming your worst fears. Then with big ballyhoo you let the boys off the hook. They happily relax into home life again; you're a big hero for not allowing a travesty of justice. We don't even need to mention Lydia was ever there, ever involved in any way. And we also don't bring up your tampering with Lowe's stash. Everybody's off the hook. All bets are off. And Lowe Acree gets to rest in peace— at whatever godforsaken level of hell he lives at now."

He thought.

But I wouldn't let him think for long. "In exchange for our silence about everything, you get to stay out of jail. But you allow the Turner boys to take Lydia home with them and you promise never, *ever* to mess with her, apart from the occasional Christmas card, ever again in your life."

Maytag popped in. "What about Ronnie?"

I looked at Tommy again. "Yeah. What about Ronnie Tibadeau? I mean, I know he was a petty criminal, but . . ."

Tommy was recovering a little of his mean-cop

persona. "I could always say I killed *him* in the line of duty."

Dally had to question that. "By running over him with a car and then handcuffing the body to the chassis? It's a stretch."

Tommy made no eye contact.

Lydia had an idea. "You give a large sum of money to his relatives out of the drug money you and Lowe made. They make a donation to the technical school in Tifton in the name of Ronnie Tibadeau, to establish scholarships—"

I had to break in. "—for auto mechanics."

She nodded. "Right."

Tommy sighed a sigh like the last breath of a dying man.

Dally filled him in. "Otherwise you die in jail."

I checked around the room with everybody. "Okay?"

Lydia was philosophical. "I just wish it could all go back to the way it was when I was little, and all this didn't really matter."

Dally smiled so sweet, you could have had it for dessert. "Flap's good, sugar, but he's already explained to me that the one thing he can't do"—she shot me a look with the eyebrow lift—"is recall a lost hour. So is this deal good enough?"

Lydia smiled. That smile was the lock on my proposition. Tommy saw it, and nodded his head. We had a deal.

43

Namesakes

As far as deals go, it worked pretty well. We pulled what was left of poor Ronnie Tibadeau out from under my car. Maytag got the handcuff key from Tommy and unlocked the body. The boys wanted to dispose of him themselves, out of respect for their boyhood acquaintance. They found, appropriately enough, an empty grave in the yard where Ida had lost her voice. They covered him up with a little dirt.

We had a short ceremony where everybody mentioned something good about the boy. I talked about my carburetor. It was very much the product of everybody's being too tired and too strange and stretched for too many hours. Lydia had a tear or two, and I have to admit to feeling pretty crummy about the kid. After all was said and done, he hadn't been a bad sort.

Then we all went back to Tifton. The Peaker Brothers handled the exhuming of Lowe's body. He was in pretty good shape, really, except for the fact that he had no pants on and was wearing boxer shorts with red hearts and Dalmatians. I got a pretty good laugh out of it, and I thought the Peakers might bust a gut slapping their thighs and whacking each other on the arm. Tommy was pretty quiet, but maybe he was remembering going fishing with Lowe as a boy.

Anyway, Lowe was found to have massive amounts of cocaine and heroin in his system. Enough to kill ten guys, they said. The report also mentioned that he'd probably been boating in the last hours before his death because of the presence in his blood of a common remedy for seasickness.

Lydia Sylvia Habersham Acree—that's the name on her police report—was the dumbfounded inheritor of what was to me a relatively mind-numbing sum of money. It was a sum so staggering to me that I figured grown men would pass out at the mention of it. So remarkable was this sum of money that the guy who was handling the transaction didn't care to even say it out loud. Seems Lowe Acree was fabulously well-to-do, as they say, and had no last will and testament when he died. So it all went to his grieving widow. She didn't seem to care much at all one way or the other. She just looked at the sum of money and smiled. Didn't seem that grandiose to her, I guess. What do I know? I get excited about a fifty-dollar bill.

Lydia paid off Dally's new club on River Street without asking, without even blinking an eye. She wanted to buy me a new car, but I told her the one I had ran just fine. She acquired Lowe's home of course. She had it demolished. There was some talk among us of salting the earth, too, but it never panned out. Lydia built a garden park on the land instead, much to the chagrin of the ritzy neighbors. Planted a lot of impatiens.

Lydia herself moved in with the Turner family. She had her own little room, and she loved to cook with Ida. And every chance she got she'd head east, to the ocean.

Except for a card every December the twenty-fifth, she was never to hear from Tommy Acree again.

And by fall quarter there was a new perpetual scholarship fund at the technical school in Tifton.

For the Turner boys nothing much changed. They were very happy to have Lydia with them whenever she could be there, and the house was filled with laughter nearly all the time. They invited me to their Thanksgiving dinner, but I couldn't make it. Maybe next time.

I did eventually get a bottle or two of Rusty's Barbecue. And despite my unshakable opinion that the word *wine* only applies if it's red and comes from France, Rusty's makes an okay after-dinner drink—like a port, only completely unsophisticated.

When I went down to pick up a case and tie up the last loose ends in Tifton that January, I happened to run into good old Pevus Arnold.

"Hey! Mr. Tucker! Hey!" He was glad to see me.

"Pevus."

"Look." He pushed a cute young girl my way. "It's my wife. You done saved her life. We went up to that Dr. Thompson like you said."

She was reverent. "He's a saint."

Pevus shrugged it off. "She likes him. Anyway, guess what? You'll never guess."

"Okay, so tell me."

"We didn't never know it, but she'd got twins."

She nodded, very proud. "We had twins."

I didn't know what to say. "Wow."

He was earnest. "Uh-huh, and if we hadn't found it out when we did, things might just of gone real bad for 'er. That's what they said at the doctor's. But thanks to you, we all gonna be just fine."

She was impatient. "Tell him."

"Oh. Okay. Well, seein' as how you got us to the doctor—and also because you saved Peachy and Maytag, which I did tell you they were my buds and it makes you a kinda local hero down here or whatnot—we think the world and all of you. So, if you don't mind—"

She couldn't wait. "We named the babies after you and Ms. Oglethorpe."

Without the least self-consciousness he added the kicker. "You a old dude, an' prob'ly ain't never gonna have none of your own, so we thought it was kind of an honor or what have you."

So, okay, then I *really* didn't know what to say. "You actually want to name your children Flap and Dalliance?"

She spoke like she was in church. "Oh, yes."

He explained it to me. "One's a boy and one's a girl, see?"

She thought about it. "They don't look much alike, for twins."

Pevus poked his wife. "I'm just thankful the girl looks like you an' not me."

She giggled. She was very content. He squeezed her. He was very happy. What could I say?

"Well . . . thanks, kids. I am honored. Dally will be too."

Pevus nodded. His work was done. They headed off around the side of the shed where Rusty kept his stuff. It was one of the images out of my little vision thing from months before.

I called out after them. "By the way? I kind of wish I'd gotten a chance to thank Ronnie for fixing my car. Runs great now. I don't ever have to stop on the side of the road anymore."

He turned and smiled softly at me. "That's good. I miss Ronnie. You know him. He's prob'ly off on some bad deed or other wherever he is. I'm happy the car still works good, though. Never can tell what kinda people might happen by when you're stranded on the side of the road."

I guess when it's all said and done, it's important to remember your family, no matter how loony they are. That's the thing about the family folklore. No matter how odd it seems, it's got to be passed down, from one person in the family to another, through time and through space. It has a reality to it that nothing else has—something you've actually touched with your own hands, or spoken with your own voice. Why do you have to do it? Because it's essential when you're trying to figure out something about yourself. And take it from me, the unexamined life is not even worth sleeping through.

But there are two kinds of families, see. One of

them you're born with. It's a biological event and there's no squawking about that, you've just got to take it. But the other kind is your spiritual family, if you don't mind my putting it that way. Those are the people you find—or the people who find you— the ones you're *supposed* to be around. Those are the people you have dinner with, the people you count on, the people you listen to when they tell their stories. In short, those are the people that something tells you to love. What else can you do?